AWAY IN
THE WILDERNESS

R.M. BALLANTYNE

Frontispiece by John Betancourt. Based on a painting.

AWAY IN
THE WILDERNESS

R.M. Ballantyne

WILDSIDE PRESS

AWAY IN
THE WILDERNESS

INTRODUCTION

Robert Michael Ballantyne (1825–1894) was a Scottish author who published more than 100 books. He was also an accomplished artist and exhibited some of his water-colours at the Royal Scottish Academy.

Ballantyne was born in Edinburgh, the ninth of ten children (and the youngest son), to Alexander and Anne Ballantyne. His father was a newspaper editor and printer in the family firm of "Ballantyne & Co" based at Paul's Works on the Canongate. His uncle, James Ballantyne, was the printer for Scottish author Sir Walter Scott. A banking crisis in 1825 resulted in the collapse of the Ballantyne printing business the following year with debts of £130,000,which led to a decline in the family's fortunes.

Robert Ballantyne went to Canada at the age of 16 and spent five years working for the Hudson's Bay Company. He traded with the local Native Americans for furs, which required him to travel by canoe and sleigh to the areas occupied by the modern-day provinces of Manitoba, Ontario, and Quebec—experiences that formed the basis of his novel *Snowflakes and Sunbeams* (1856). His longing for family and home during that period impressed him to start writing letters to his mother. Ballantyne recalled in his autobiographical *Personal Reminiscences in Book Making* (1893) that "To this long-letter writing I attribute whatever small amount of facility in composition I may have acquired."

In 1847 Ballantyne returned to Scotland to discover that his father had died. He published his first book the following year, *Hudson's Bay: or, Life in the Wilds of North America*, and for some time was employed by the publishers Messrs Constable. In 1856 he gave up business to focus on his literary career and began the series of adventure stories for the young with which his name is popularly associated.

The Young Fur-Traders (1856), *The Coral Island* (1857), *The World of Ice* (1859), *Ungava: a Tale of Eskimo Land* (1857), *The Dog*

Crusoe (1860), *The Lighthouse* (1865), *Fighting the Whales* (1866), *Deep Down* (1868), *The Pirate City* (1874), *Erling the Bold* (1869), *The Settler and the Savage* (1877), and more than 100 other books followed in regular succession, his rule being to write as far as possible from personal knowledge of the scenes he described. *The Gorilla Hunters: A tale of the wilds of Africa* (1861) shares three characters with The Coral Island: Jack Martin, Ralph Rover and Peterkin Gay. Here Ballantyne relied factually on Paul du Chaillu's Exploration in Equatorial Guinea, which had appeared early in the same year.

The Coral Island remains the most popular of the Ballantyne novels still read and remembered today, but because of a mistake he made in that book—he gave an incorrect thickness of coconut shells—he prioritized research on his subjects for later books. For instance, he spent time living with the lighthouse keepers at the Bell Rock before writing *The Lighthouse*, and he spent time with the tin miners of Cornwall while researching *Deep Down*.

In 1866 he married Jane Grant, with whom he had three sons and three daughters. He spent his later years in Harrow, London, before moving to Italy for the sake of his health, possibly suffering from undiagnosed Ménière's disease. He died in Rome in 1894 and was buried in the Protestant Cemetery there.

One of the young men influenced by Ballantyne's novels was Robert Louis Stevenson (1850–94). Stevenson was so impressed with the story of *The Coral Island* (1857) that he based portions of his most famous book, *Treasure Island* (1881), on themes found in Ballantyne's classic novel.

—Karl Wurf
Rockville, Maryland

CHAPTER I.

The Hunter.

On a beautiful summer evening, not many years ago, a man was seen to ascend the side of a little mound or hillock, on the top of which he lingered to gaze upon the wild scenery that lay stretched out before him.

The man wore the leathern coat and leggings of a North American hunter, or trapper, or backwoodsman; and well did he deserve all these titles, for Jasper Derry was known to his friends as the best hunter, the most successful trapper, and the boldest man in the backwoods.

Jasper was big and strong as well as bold, but he was not a bully. Men of true courage are in general peacefully disposed. Jasper could fight like a lion when there was occasion to do so; but he was gentle and grave, and quiet by nature. He was also extremely good-humoured; had a low soft voice, and, both in mind and body, seemed to delight in a state of repose.

We have said that his coat was made of leather; the moccasins or Indian shoes on his feet were made of the same material. When Jasper first put them on they were soft like a glove of chamois leather, and bright yellow; but hard service had turned them into a dirty brown, which looked more business like. The sun had burned his face and hands to as deep a brown as his coat. On his head he wore a little round cap, which he had made with his own hands, after having caught the black fox that supplied the fur, in one of his own traps. A coloured worsted belt bound his coat round his waist, and beneath the coat he wore a scarlet flannel shirt. A long knife and a small hatchet were stuck in the belt at his back, and in front hung a small cloth bag, which was so thickly ornamented with beads of many colours, that little of the cloth could be seen.

This last was a fire-bag — so called because it contained the flint, steel, and tinder required for making a fire. It also contained Jasper's pipe and tobacco — for he smoked, as a matter of course. Men smoke everywhere — more's the pity — and Jasper followed the example of those around him. Smoking was almost his only fault. He was a tremendous smoker. Often, when out of tobacco, he had smoked tea. Frequently he had tried bark and dried leaves; and once, when hard pressed, he had smoked oakum. He would rather have gone without his supper than without his pipe! A powder-horn and shot pouch were slung over his shoulders by two cross belts, and he carried a long single-barrelled gun.

I have been thus particular in describing Jasper Derry, because he is our hero, and he is worth describing, being a fine, hearty, handsome fellow, who cared as little for a wild Indian or a grizzly bear as he did for a butterfly, and who was one of the best of companions, as he was one of the best of hunters, in the wilderness.

Having gained the top of the hillock, Jasper placed the butt of his long gun on the ground, and, crossing his hands over the muzzle, stood there for some time so motionless, that he might have been mistaken for a statue. A magnificent country was spread out before him. Just in front lay a clear lake of about a mile in extent, and the evening was so still that every tree, stone, and bush on its margin, was reflected as in a mirror. Here, hundreds of wild ducks and wild geese were feeding among the sedges of the bays, or flying to and fro mingling their cries with those of thousands of plover and other kinds of water-fowl that inhabited the place. At the lower end of this lake a small rivulet was seen to issue forth and wind its way through woods and plains like a silver thread, until it was lost to view in the far distance. On the right and left and behind, the earth was covered with the dense foliage of the wild woods.

The hillock on which the western hunter stood, lay in the very heart of that great uncultivated wilderness which forms part of the British possessions in North America. This region lies to the north of the Canadas, is nearly as large as all Europe, and goes by the name of the Hudson's Bay Territory, or Rupert's Land.

It had taken Jasper many long weeks of hard travel by land and water, in canoes and on foot, to get there; and several weeks of toil still lay before him ere he could attain the object for which his journey had been undertaken.

Wicked people say that "woman is at the bottom of all mischief!" Did it never occur to these same wicked individuals, that woman is just as much at the bottom of all good? Whether for good or for evil, woman was at the bottom of Jasper Perry's heart and affairs. The cause of his journey was love; the aim and end of it was marriage! Did true love ever run smooth? "No, never," says the proverb. We shall see.

CHAPTER II.

The Three Friends.

When the hunter had stood for full five minutes gazing at the beautiful scenery by which he was surrounded, it suddenly occurred to him that a pipe would render him much more capable of enjoying it; so he sat down on the trunk of a fallen tree, leaned his gun on it, pulled the fire-bag from his belt, and began to fill his pipe, which was one of the kind used by the savages of the country, with a stone head and a wooden stem. It was soon lighted, and Jasper was thinking how much more clear and beautiful a landscape looked through tobacco smoke, when a hand was laid lightly on his shoulder. Looking quickly round, he beheld a tall dark-faced Indian standing by his side.

Jasper betrayed neither alarm nor surprise; for the youth was his own comrade, who had merely come to tell him that the canoe in which they had been travelling together, and which had been slightly damaged, was repaired and ready for service.

"Why, Arrowhead, you steal on me with the soft tread of a fox. My ears are not dull, yet I did not hear your approach, lad."

A smile lighted up the countenance of the young Indian for a moment, as he listened to a compliment which gratified him much; but the grave expression which was natural to him instantly returned, as he said, "Arrowhead has hunted in the Rocky Mountains where the men are treacherous; he has learned to tread lightly there."

"No doubt, ye had need to be always on the look out where there are such varmints; but hereaway, Arrowhead, there are no foes to fear, and therefore no need to take yer friends by surprise. But ye're proud o' your gifts, lad, an' I suppose it's natural to like to show them off. Is the canoe ready?"

The Indian replied by a nod.

"That's well, lad, it will be sun-down in another hour, an' I would like to camp on the point of pines to-night; so come along."

"Hist!" exclaimed the Indian, pointing to a flock of geese which came into view at that moment.

"Ah! you come of a masterful race," said Jasper, shaking his head gravely, "you're never content when ye've got enough, but must always be killing God's creatures right and left for pure sport. Haven't we got one grey goose already for supper, an' that's enough for two men surely. Of course I make no account o' the artist, poor cratur', for he eats next to nothin'. Hows'ever, as your appetite may be sharper set than usual, I've no objection to bring down another for ye."

So saying the hunter and the Indian crouched behind a bush, and the former, while he cocked his gun and examined the priming, gave utterance to a series of cries so loud and discordant, that any one who was ignorant of a hunter's ways must have thought he was anxious to drive all the living creatures within six miles of him away in terror. Jasper had no such wish, however. He was merely imitating the cry of the wild geese. The birds, which were at first so far-off that a rifle-ball could not have reached them, no sooner heard the cry of their friends (as they doubtless thought it) than they turned out of their course, and came gradually towards the bush where the two men lay hidden.

The hunter did not cease to cry until the birds were within gunshot. Then he fixed his eye on one of the flock that seemed plump and fat. The long barrel of the gun was quickly raised, the geese discovered their mistake, and the whole flock were thrown into wild confusion as they attempted to sheer off; but it was too late. Smoke and fire burst from the bush, and an enormous grey goose fell with a heavy crash to the ground.

"What have you shot? what have you shot?" cried a shrill and somewhat weak voice in the distance. In another moment the owner of the voice appeared, running eagerly towards the two men.

"Use your eyes, John Heywood, an' ye won't need to ask," said Jasper, with a quiet smile, as he carefully reloaded his gun.

"Ah! I see — a grey swan — no, surely, it cannot be a goose?" said Heywood, turning the bird over and regarding it with astonishment; "why, this is the biggest one I ever did see."

"What's yon in the water? Deer, I do believe," cried Jasper, quickly drawing the small shot from his gun and putting in a ball instead. "Come, lads, we shall have venison for supper to-night. That beast can't reach t'other side so soon as we can."

Jasper leaped quickly down the hill, and dashed through the bushes towards the spot where their canoe lay. He was closely followed by his companions, and in less than two minutes they were darting across the lake in their little Indian canoe, which was made of birch-bark, and was so light that one man could carry it easily.

While they are thus engaged I will introduce the reader to

John Heywood. This individual was a youth of nineteen or twenty years of age, who was by profession a painter of landscapes and animals. He was tall and slender in person, with straight black hair, a pale haggard-looking face, an excitable nervous manner, and an enthusiastic temperament. Being adventurous in his disposition, he had left his father's home in Canada, and entreated his friend, Jasper Derry, to take him along with him into the wilderness. At first Jasper was very unwilling to agree to this request; because the young artist was utterly ignorant of everything connected with a life in the woods, and he could neither use a paddle nor a gun. But Heywood's father had done him some service at a time when he was ill and in difficulties, so, as the youth was very anxious to go, he resolved to repay this good turn of the father by doing a kindness to the son.

Heywood turned out but a poor backwoodsman, but he proved to be a pleasant, amusing companion, and as Jasper and the Indian were quite sufficient for the management of the light canoe, and the good gun of the former was more than sufficient to feed the party, it mattered nothing to Jasper that Heywood spent most of his time seated in the middle of the canoe, sketching the scenery as they went along. Still less did it matter that Heywood missed everything he fired at, whether it was close at hand or far away.

At first Jasper was disposed to look upon his young companion as a poor useless creature; and the Indian regarded him with undisguised contempt. But after they had been some time in his company, the opinions of these two men of the woods changed; for they found that the artist was wise, and well informed on many subjects of which they were extremely ignorant; and they beheld with deep admiration the beautiful and life-like drawings and paintings which he produced in rapid succession.

Such was the romantic youth who had, for the sake of seeing and painting the wilderness, joined himself to these rough sons of the forest, and who now sat in the centre of the canoe swaying his arms about and shouting with excitement as they quickly drew near to the swimming herd of deer.

"Keep yourself still," said Jasper, looking over his shoulder, "ye'll upset the canoe if ye go on like that."

"Give me the axe, give me the axe, I'll kill him!" cried Heywood.

"Take your pencil and draw him," observed the hunter, with a quiet laugh. "Now, Arrowhead, two good strokes of the paddle will do — there — so."

As he spoke the canoe glanced up alongside of an affrighted deer, and in the twinkling of an eye Jasper's long knife was in its heart, and the water was dyed with blood. This happened quite near to the opposite shore of the lake, so that in little more than half an hour after it was killed the animal was cut up and packed, and the canoe was again speeding towards the upper end of the lake, where the party arrived just as night began to fling its dark mantle over the wilderness.

CHAPTER III.

The Encampment.

Camping out in the woods at night is truly a delightful thing, and the pleasantest part of it, perhaps, is the lighting of the fire. Light is agreeable to human eyes and cheering to the human heart. Solomon knew and felt that when he penned the words, "A pleasant thing it is for the eyes to behold the sun." And the rising of the sun is scarcely more grateful to the feelings than the lighting of a fire on a dark night. So our friends thought and felt, when the fire blazed up, but they were too busy and too hungry at the time to think about the state of their feelings.

The Indian was hungry. A good fire had to be made before the venison could be roasted, so he gave his whole attention to the felling of dry trees and cutting them up into logs for the fire. Jasper was also hungry, and a slight shower had wetted all the moss and withered grass, so he had enough to do to strike fire with flint and steel, catch a spark on a little piece of tinder, and then blow and coax the spark into a flame.

The artist was indeed free to indulge in a little meditation; but he had stumbled in the dark on landing, and bruised his shins, so he could only sit down on a rock and rub them and feel miserable.

But the fire soon caught; branches were heaped up, great logs were piled on, forked tongues of flame began to leap up and lick the branches of the overhanging trees. The green leaves looked rich and warm; the thick stems looked red and hot; the faces and clothes of the men seemed as if about to catch fire as they moved about the encampment preparing supper. In short, the whole scene was so extremely comfortable, in reality as well as in appearance, that Heywood forgot his bruised shins and began to rub his hands with delight.

In a very short time three juicy venison-steaks were steaming before the three travellers, and in a much shorter time they had disappeared altogether and were replaced by three new ones. The mode of cooking was very simple. Each steak was fixed on a piece of stick and set up before the fire to roast. When one side was ready, the artist, who seemed to have very little patience, began to cut off pieces and eat them while the other side was cooking.

To say truth, men out in those regions have usually such good appetites that they are not particular as to the cooking of their food. Quantity, not quality, is what they desire. They generally feel very much like the Russian, of whom it is said, that he would be content to eat sawdust if only he *got plenty of it*! The steaks were washed down with tea. There is no other drink in Rupert's Land. The Hudson's Bay Company found that spirits were so hurtful to the Indians that they refused to send them into the country; and at the present day there is no strong drink to be had for love or money over the length and breadth of their territories, except at those places where other fur-traders oppose them, and oblige them, in self-defence, to sell fire-water, as the Indians call it.

Tea is the great — the only — drink in Rupert's Land! Yes,

laugh as ye will, ye lovers of gin and beer and whisky, one who has tried it, and has seen it tried by hundreds of stout stalwart men, tells you that the teetotaller is the best man for real hard work.

The three travellers drank their tea and smacked their lips, and grinned at each other with great satisfaction. They could not have done more if it had been the best of brandy and they the jolliest of topers! But the height of their enjoyment was not reached until the pipes were lighted.

It was quite a sight to see them smoke! Jasper lay with his huge frame extended in front of the blaze, puffing clouds of smoke thick enough to have shamed a small cannon. Arrow-head rested his back on the stump of a tree, stretched his feet towards the fire, and allowed the smoke to roll slowly through his nostrils as well as out at his mouth, so that it kept curling quietly round his nose, and up his cheeks, and into his eyes, and through his hair in a most delightful manner; at least so it would seem, for his reddish-brown face beamed with happy contentment.

Young Heywood did not smoke, but he drew forth his sketch-book and sketched his two companions; and in the practice of his beloved art, I have no doubt, he was happier than either.

"I wonder how many trading-posts the Hudson's Bay Company has got?" said Heywood, as he went on with his work.

"Hundreds of 'em," said Jasper, pressing the red-hot tobacco into the bowl of his pipe with the end of his little finger, as slowly and coolly as if his flesh were fire-proof. "I don't know, exactly, how many they've got. I doubt if anybody does, but they have them all over the country. You've seen a little of the country now, Heywood; well, what you have seen is very much like what you will see as long as you choose to travel hereaway. You come to a small clearing in the forest, with five or six log houses in it, a stockade round it, and a flag-staff in the middle of it; five, ten, or fifteen men, and a gentleman in charge. That's a Hudson's Bay Company's trading-post. All round it lie the wild woods. Go through the woods for two or three hundred miles and you'll come to another such post, or fort, as we sometimes call 'em. That's how it is all the country over. Although there are many of them, the country is so uncommon big that they may be said to be few and far between. Some are bigger and some are less. There's scarcely a settlement in the country worthy o' the name of a village except Red River."

"Ah! Red River," exclaimed Heywood, "I've heard much of that settlement — hold steady — I'm drawing your *nose* just now — have you been there, Jasper?"

"That have I, lad, and a fine place it is, extendin' fifty miles or more along the river, with fine fields, and handsome houses, and churches, and missionaries and schools, and what not; but the rest of Rupert's Land is just what you have seen; no roads, no houses, no cultivated fields — nothing but lakes, and rivers, and woods, and plains without end, and a few Indians here and there, with plenty of wild beasts everywhere. These trading-posts are scattered here and there, from the Atlantic to the Pacific, and from Canada to the Frozen Sea, standin' solitary-like in the midst of the wilderness, as if they had dropped down from the clouds by mistake and didn't know exactly what to do with themselves."

"How long have de Company lived?" inquired Arrowhead, turning suddenly to Jasper.

The stout hunter felt a little put out. "Ahem! I don't exactly know; but it must have been a long time, no doubt."

"Oh, I can tell you that," cried Heywood.

"You?" said Jasper in surprise.

"Ay; the Company was started nearly two hundred years ago by Prince Rupert, who was the first Governor, and that's the reason the country came to be called Rupert's Land. You know its common name is 'the Hudson's Bay Territory,' because it surrounds Hudson's Bay."

"Why, where did you learn that?" said Jasper, "I thought I knowed a-most everything about the Company; but I must confess I never knew that about Prince Rupert before."

"I learned it from books," said the artist.

"Books!" exclaimed Jasper, "I never learned nothin' from books — more's the pity. I git along well enough in the trappin' and shootin' way without 'em; but I'm sorry I never learned to read. Ah! I've a great opinion of books — so I have."

The worthy hunter shook his head solemnly as he said this in a low voice, more to himself than to his companions, and he continued to mutter and shake his head for some minutes, while he knocked the ashes out of his pipe. Having refilled and relighted it, he drew his blanket over his shoulder, laid his head upon a tuft of grass, and continued to smoke until he fell asleep, and allowed the pipe to fall from his lips.

The Indian followed his example, with this difference, that he laid aside his pipe, and drew the blanket over his head and under his feet, and wrapped it round him in such a way that he resembled a man sewed up in a sack.

Heywood was thus compelled to shut his sketch-book; so he also wrapped himself in his blanket, and was soon sound asleep.

The camp-fire gradually sank low. Once or twice the end of a log fell, sending up a bright flame and a shower of sparks, which, for a few seconds, lighted up the scene again and revealed the three slumbering figures. But at last the fire died out altogether, and left the encampment in such thick darkness that the sharpest eye would have failed to detect the presence of man in that distant part of the lone wilderness.

CHAPTER IV.

Mosquitoes — Camp-Fire Talk.

There is a certain fly in the American forests which is worthy of notice, because it exercises a great influence over the happiness of man in those regions. This fly is found in many other parts of the world, but it swarms in immense numbers in America, particularly in the swampy districts of that continent, and in the hot months of summer. It is called a mosquito — pronounced *moskeeto* — and it is, perhaps, the most tormenting, the most persevering, savage, vicious little monster on the face of the earth. Other flies go to sleep at night; the mosquito never does. Darkness puts down other flies — it seems to encourage the mosquito. Day and night it persecutes man and beast, and the only time of the twenty-four hours in which it seems to rest is about noon, when the heat puts *it* down for a little. But this period of rest strengthens it for a renewal of war during the remainder of the day and night. In form the mosquito very much resembles the gnat, but is somewhat larger. This instrument of torture is his nose, which is quite as long as his body, and sharper than the finest needle. Being unable to rest because of the mosquitoes, Heywood resolved to have a chat.

"Come, Jasper," said he, looking up into his companion's grave countenance, "although we have been many weeks on this journey now, you have not yet told me what has brought you here, or what the end of your trip is going to be."

"I've come here a-hunting," said Jasper, with the look and tone of a man who did not wish to be questioned.

"Nay, now, I know that is not the reason," said Heywood, smiling; "you could have hunted much nearer home, if you had been so minded, and to as good purpose. Come, Jasper, you know I'm your friend, and that I wish you well. Let me hear what has brought you so far into the wilderness — mayhap I can give you some good advice if you do."

"Well, lad, I don't mind if I do. Though, for the matter of good advice, I don't feel much in need of any just at this time."

Jasper shook the ashes out of his pipe, and refilled it as he spoke; then he shook his head once or twice and smiled, as if his thoughts amused him. Having lighted the pipe, he stretched himself out in a more comfortable way before the blaze, and said —

"Well, lad, I'll tell ye what it is — it's the old story; the love of woman has brought me here."

"And a very good old story it is," returned Heywood, with a look of interest. "A poor miserable set of creatures we should be without that same love of woman. Come, Jasper, I'm glad to hear you're such a sensible fellow. I know something about that subject myself. There's a pretty blue-eyed girl, with golden hair, down away in Canada that —" Heywood stopped short in his speech and sighed.

"Come, it ain't a hopeless case, is it?" said Jasper, with a look of sympathy.

"I rather fear it is; but I hope not. Ah, what should we do

without hope in this world?"

"That's true," observed Jasper, with much gravity, "we could not get on at all without hope."

"But come, Jasper," said the artist, "let's hear about your affair, and I'll tell you about mine some other time."

"Well, there is not much to tell, but I'll give ye all that's of it. You must know, then, that about two years ago I was in the service of the Hudson's Bay Company, at one o' their outposts in the McKenzie's River district. We had little to eat there and little to do, and I felt so lonesome, never seein' a human bein' except the four or five men at the fort an' a few Indians, that I made up my mind to quit. I had no reason to complain o' the Company, d'ye see. They always treated me handsomely, and it was no fault o' theirs that the livin' in that district was poor and the post lonesome.

"Well, on my way down to Lake Winnipeg, I fell in with a brigade o' boats goin' to the Saskatchewan district, and we camped together that night. One o' the guides of the Saskatchewan brigade had his daughter with him. The guide was a French-Canadian, and his wife had been a Scotch half-caste, so what the daughter was is more than I can tell; but I know what she looked like. She just looked like an angel. It wasn't so much that she was pretty, but she was so sweet, and so quiet lookin', and so innocent! Well, to cut the matter short, I fell in love at once. D'ye know what it is, Heywood, to fall in love at first sight?"

"Oh! don't I?" replied the artist with sudden energy.

"An' d'ye know," continued Jasper, "what it is to be fallen-in-love-with, at first sight?"

"Well, no, I'm not so sure about that," replied Heywood sadly.

"I do, then," said Jasper, "for that sweet critter fell in love with me right off — though what she saw in me to love has puzzled me much. Howsoever, she did, and for that I'm thankful. Her name is Marie Laroche. She and I opened our minds to each other that night, and I took the guide, her father, into the woods, and told him I wanted his daughter; and he was agreeable; but he would not hear of my takin' her away then and there. He told me I must go down to Canada and get settled, and when I had a house to put his daughter in, I was to come back into the wilderness here and be married to her, and then take her home — so here I am on my way to claim my bride. But there's one thing that puzzles me sorely."

"What is that?" asked Heywood.

"I've never heard from Marie from that day to this," said Jasper.

"That is strange," replied the other; "but perhaps she cannot write."

"That's true. Now, you speak of it, I do believe she can't write a line; but, then, she might have got some one to write for her."

"Did you leave your address with her?"

"How could I, when I had no address to leave?"

"But did you ever send it to her?"

"No, I never thought of that," said Jasper, opening his eyes very wide. "Come, that's a comfort — that's a good reason for never havin' heard from her. Thankee, lad, for putting me up to it. And, now, as we must be up and away in another hour, I'll finish my nap."

So saying, Jasper put out his pipe and once more drew his blanket over him. Heywood followed his example, and while he lay there gazing up at the stars through the trees, he heard the worthy hunter muttering to himself, "That's it; that accounts for my not hearin' from her."

A sigh followed the words, very soon a snore followed the sigh, and ere many minutes had passed away, the encampment was again buried in darkness and repose.

CHAPTER V.

Journeying in the Wilderness.

It seemed to Heywood that he had not been asleep more than five minutes, when he was aroused by Jasper laying his heavy hand on his shoulder. On rubbing his eyes and gazing round him, he found that the first streak of dawn was visible in the eastern sky, that the canoe was already in the water, and that his companions were ready to embark.

It is usually found that men are not disposed to talk at that early hour. Heywood merely remarked that it was a fine morning, to which Jasper replied by a nod of his head. Nothing more was said. The artist rolled up his blanket in a piece of oiled-cloth, collected his drawing materials and put them into their bag, got into his place in the centre of the canoe, and immediately went to sleep, while Jasper and the Indian, taking their places in the bow and stern, dipped the paddles into the water and shot away from the shore. They looked mysterious and ghostly in the dim morning light; and the whole scene around them looked mysterious and ghostly too, for the water in the lake seemed black, and the shores and islands looked like dark shadows, and a pale thin mist rolled slowly over the surface of the water and hung overhead. No sound was heard except the light plash of the paddles as the two backwoodsmen urged their little canoe swiftly along.

By degrees the light of day increased, and Jasper awakened Heywood in order that he might behold the beautiful scenery through which they passed. They were now approaching the upper end of the lake, in which there were innumerable islands of every shape and size – some of them not more than a few yards in length, while some were two or three hundred yards across, but all were clothed with the most beautiful green foliage and shrubbery. As the pale yellow of the eastern sky began to grow red, ducks and gulls bestirred themselves. Early risers among them first began to chirp, and scream, and whistle their morning song, – for there are lazy ones among the birds, just as there are among men. Sometimes, when the canoe rounded a point of rocks a flock of geese were found floating peacefully among the sedges, sound asleep, with their heads under their wings. These would leap into the air and fly off in great alarm, with much difficulty and tremendous splutter, reminding one of the proverb, "The more haste the less speed." At other times they would come upon a flock of ducks so suddenly, that they had no time to take wing, so they dived instead, and thus got out of the way.

Then the yellow hue of sunrise came, a good while before the sun himself rose. The last of the bright stars were put out by the flood of light, and multitudes of little birds on shore began to chirp their morning song; and who can say that this was not a hymn of praise to God, when, in the Holy Bible itself, in the 150th Psalm, we find it written, "Let everything that hath breath praise the Lord."

At last the sun burst forth in all his golden glory. Water, earth, and sky glowed as if they had been set on fire. What a blessed influence the sun has upon this world! It resembles the countenance of a loving father beaming in upon his family, driving away clouds, and diffusing warmth and joy.

The birds were now all astir together, insomuch that the air seemed alive with them. There are small white gulls, with red legs and red beaks, in those large inland lakes, just as there are on the ocean. These began to utter their sweet wild cries so powerfully that they almost drowned the noise of all the rest. Yet the united chorus of the whole was not harsh. It was softened and mellowed by distance, and fell on the ears of the two hunters as pleasantly as the finest music does in the ears of men trained to sweet sounds from infancy.

Not until the sun had ascended a considerable way on its course through the sky, did Jasper think it necessary to lay down his paddle. By that time the upper end of the lake had been reached, and the hunter had run the canoe close to a ledge of flat rock and jumped ashore, saying that it was time for breakfast.

"I had almost got to believe I was in paradise," said Heywood, as he stepped ashore.

"I often think there's a good deal of the garden of Eden still left in this world," replied Jasper, as he carried the kettle up to the level part of the rock and began to kindle a fire, while the Indian, as usual, hewed the wood. "If we could only make use of God's gifts instead of abusin' them, I do believe we might be very happy all our days."

"See there, Jasper, is one of the birds I want so much to get hold of. I want to make a drawing of him. Would you object to spend a shot on such game."

Heywood pointed as he spoke to a grey bird, about the size of a blackbird, which sat on a branch close above his head. This creature is called by the fur-traders a whisky-John, and it is one of the most impudent little birds in the world! Wherever you go throughout the country, there you find whisky-Johns ready to receive and welcome you, as if they were the owners of the soil. They are perfectly fearless; they will come and sit on a branch within a yard of your hand, when you are eating, and look at you in the most inquisitive manner. If they could speak, they could not say more plainly, "What have you got there? – give me some!" If you leave the mouth of your provision sack open they are sure to jump into it. When you are done eating they will scarcely let you six yards away before they make a dash at the crumbs; and if you throw sticks or stones at them, they will hop out of the way, but they will not take to flight!

"It would be a pity to waste powder on them critters," said Jasper, "but I'll catch one for you."

As he said this he took a few crumbs of broken meat from the bottom of the provision sack and spread them on his right hand; then he lay down under a bush, covered his face with a few leaves, and thrust out his hand. Heywood and the Indian retired a few paces and stood still to await the result.

In a few seconds a whisky-John came flying towards the open hand, and alighted on a branch within a yard of it. Here he shook his feathers and looked very bold, but suspicious, for a few minutes, turning first one eye towards the hand, and then the other. After a little he hopped on a branch still nearer, and, seeing no motion in the hand, he at last hopped upon the palm and began to peck the crumbs. Instantly the fingers closed, and Jasper caught him by the toes, whereupon the whisky-John began to scream furiously with rage and terror. But I am bound to say there was more of rage than of terror in his cry.

Jasper handed the passionate bird over to the artist, who tried to make a portrait of him, but he screamed and pecked so fiercely that Heywood was obliged to let him go after making a rough sketch.

Breakfast was a repetition of the supper of the night before; it was soon disposed of, and the three travellers again set forth. This time Jasper sang one of the beautiful canoe songs peculiar to that country, and Heywood and Arrowhead, both of whom had good voices, joined in the chorus.

They soon passed from the lake into the river by which it was fed. At first the current of this river was sluggish; but as they ascended, it became stronger, and was broken here and there by rapids.

The severe toil of travelling in the backwoods now began. To paddle on a level lake all day is easy enough, for, when you get tired, you can lay down the paddle and rest. But in the river this is impossible, because of the current. The only way to get a rest is to push the bow of the canoe ashore. It was a fine sight to see the movements of Jasper and the Indian when they came to the first rapid. Heywood knew that he could be of no use, so, like a wise man, he sat still and looked on.

The rapid was a very strong one, but there were no falls in it; only a furious gush of water over the broken bed of the river, where many large rocks rose up and caught the current, hurling the water back in white foam. Any one who knew not what these hunters could do, would have laughed if you had told him they were about to ascend that rapid in such an egg-shell of a canoe!

They began by creeping up, in-shore, as far as they could. Then they dashed boldly out into the stream, and the current whirled them down with lightning speed, but suddenly the canoe came to a halt in the very middle of the stream! Every rock in a rapid has a long tail of still water below it; the canoe had got into one of these tails or eddies, and there it rested securely. A few yards higher up there was another rock, nearer to the opposite bank, and the eddy which tailed off from it came down a little lower than the rock behind which the canoe now lay. There was a furious gush of water between them and this eddy, but the men knew what the canoe could bear, and their nerves were strong and steady. Across they went like a shot. They were swept down to the extreme point of the eddy, but a few powerful strokes of the paddle sent them into it, and next moment they were floating behind the second rock, a few yards higher up the stream.

Thus they darted from rock to rock, gaining a few yards at each dart, until at last they swept into the smooth water at the head of the rapid.

Many a time was this repeated that day, for rapids were numerous; their progress was therefore slow. Sometimes they came to parts of the river where the stream was very strong and deep, but not broken by rocks, so that they had no eddies to dart into. In such places Arrowhead and Heywood walked along the bank, and hauled the canoe up by means of a line, while Jasper remained in it to steer. This was hard work, for the banks in places were very steep, in some parts composed of soft mud, into which the men sank nearly up to their knees, and in other places covered so thickly with bushes that it was almost impossible to force a path through them. Jasper and the Indian took the steering-paddle by turns, and when Heywood required a rest he got into his place in the middle of the canoe; but they never halted for more than a few minutes at a time. All day they paddled and dragged the canoe slowly up against the strong current, and when night closed in they found they had advanced only three miles on their journey.

The last obstacle they came to that day was a roaring waterfall about thirty feet high. Here, it might have been thought, was an effectual check to them at last. Nothing without wings could have gone up that waterfall, which filled the woods with the thunder of its roar; but the canoe had no wings, so what was to be done?

To one ignorant of the customs of that country, going on would have seemed impossible, but nothing can stop the advance of a backwoods voyager. If his canoe won't carry him, he carries his canoe! Jasper and his friends did so on the present occasion. They had reached what is called a portage or carrying-place, and there are hundreds of such places all over Rupert's Land.

On arriving at the foot of the fall, Heywood set off at once to a spot from which he could obtain a good view of it, and sat down to sketch, while his companions unloaded the canoe and lifted it out of the water. Then Jasper collected together as much of the baggage as he could carry, and clambered up the bank with it, until he reached the still water at the top of the fall. Here he laid it down and returned for another load. Meanwhile Arrowhead lifted the canoe with great ease, placed it on his shoulders, and bore it to the same place. When all had been carried up, the canoe was launched into the quiet water a few hundred yards above the fall, the baggage was replaced in it, and the travellers were ready to continue their voyage. This whole operation is called *making a portage*. It took about an hour to make this portage.

Portages vary in length and in numbers. In some rivers they are few and far between; in others they are so numerous that eight or twelve may have to be made in a day. Many of the portages are not more than an eighth of a mile in length, and are crossed for the purpose of avoiding a waterfall. Some are four or five miles in extent, for many long reaches in the rivers are so broken by falls and rapids, that the voyagers find it their best plan to take canoes and baggage on their backs and cut across country for several miles; thus they avoid rough places altogether.

Jasper delayed starting for half an hour, in order to give Heywood time to finish his sketch of the fall. It began to grow dark when they again embarked, so, after paddling up stream until a convenient place was found, they put ashore and encamped within sight of another waterfall, the roar of which, softened by distance, fell upon their ears all that night like the sound of pleasant music.

CHAPTER VI.

The Outpost.

On the morning of the second day after the events which I have described in the last chapter, our three travellers arrived at one of the solitary outposts belonging to the fur-traders. It stood on the banks of the river, and consisted of four small houses made of logs. It covered about an acre of ground, and its only defence was a wall of wooden posts, about two inches apart, which completely surrounded the buildings.

"This fort is a namesake of mine," said Jasper, when they first sighted it; "they call it Jasper's House. I spent a day at it when I was hereaway two years ago."

"Who is in charge of it?" asked Heywood.

"A gentleman named Grant, I believe," replied Jasper. "That white painted house in the middle of the square is his. The other house on the right, painted yellow, is where the men live. Mr. Grant has only got six men, poor fellow, to keep him company; he seldom sees a new face here from one end of the year to the other. But he makes a trip once a year to the head post of the district with his furs, and that's a sort of break to him."

"Are there no women at the place?" inquired the artist.

"Only two," replied Jasper. "At least there were two when I was here last; they were the wives of two of the men, Indian women they were, with few brains, and little or nothin' to say; but they were useful critters for all that, for they could make coats, and trousers, and moccasins, and mittens, and they were first-rate cooks, besides bein' handy at almost every kind o' work. They could even use the gun. I've heard o' them bringin' down a wild goose on the wing, when none o' the men were at hand to let drive at the passing flock. I do believe that's Mr. Grant himself standin' at the gate o' the fort."

Jasper was right. The master of Jasper's House, a big, hearty-looking man of about five-and-forty, was standing at the gate of his lonely residence, leaning against one of the door-posts, with his hands in his breeches pockets and a short pipe in his mouth. His summer employments had come to an end, — no Indians had been near the place for many weeks, and he happened to have nothing at that time to do but eat, smoke, and sleep; which three occupations he usually attended to with much earnestness. Mr. Grant did not observe the canoe approaching from below, for at that time his attention was attracted to something up the river. Suddenly he started, took his pipe from his lips, and, bending forward, listened with deep, earnest attention. A faint murmur came floating down on the breeze, sending a thrill of pleasure to the heart of the solitary man, as well it might, for a new face was a rare sight at Jasper's House.

At last a loud shout rang through the forest, and five Indian canoes swept round a point of rocks, and came suddenly into view, the men tossing their paddles in the air and sending rainbows of spray over their heads as they made for the landing-place. These were three or four families of Indians, who had come from a long hunting expedition laden with rich furs.

Their canoes, though small and light, could hold a wonderful quantity. In the foremost sat a young savage, with a dark-brown face, glittering black eyes, and stiff black hair hanging straight down all round his head, except in front, where it was cut short off just above the eyes in order to let his face appear. That fellow's canoe, besides himself, carried his three wives — he was a good hunter, and could afford to have three. Had he been a bad hunter, he would have had to content himself, poor fellow, with one! The canoe also contained six or seven heavy packs of furs; a haunch of venison; six pairs of rabbits; several ducks and geese; a lump of bear's meat; two little boys and a girl; a large tent made of deer-skins; four or five tin kettles; two or three dirty-looking dogs and a gun; several hatchets and a few blankets; two babies and a dead beaver.

In short, there was almost no end to what that bark canoe could hold; yet that Indian, with the stiff black hair, could lift it off the ground, when empty, lay it on his shoulders, and carry it for miles through the forest. The other canoes were much the same as this one.

In a few minutes they were at the bank, close under the fort, and about the same time Jasper and his friends leaped ashore, and were heartily welcomed by Mr. Grant, who was glad enough to see Indians, but was overjoyed to meet with white men.

"Glad to see you, Jasper," cried Mr. Grant, shaking the hunter by the hand; "right glad to see you. It does good to a man to see an old friend like you turn up so unexpectedly. Happy, also, to meet with you, Mr. Heywood. It's a pleasure I don't often have, to meet with a white stranger in this wilderness. Pray, come with me to the house."

The fur-trader turned to the Indians, and, saying a few

words to them in their own language, led the way to his residence.

Meanwhile, the Indians had tossed everything out of the canoes upon the bank, and the spot which had been so quiet and solitary half an hour before, became a scene of the utmost animation and confusion. While the women were employed in erecting the tents, the men strode up to the hall of reception, where Mr. Grant supplied them with tobacco and food to their hearts' content.

These natives, who, owing to the reddish copper-colour of their skins, are called red-men, — were dressed chiefly in clothes made of deer-skin; cut much in the same fashion as the garments worn by Jasper Derry. The women wore short gowns, also made of leather, and leggings of the same material; but it was noticeable that the women had leggings more ornamented with gay beads than those of the men, and they wore gaudy kerchiefs round their necks.

These women were poor looking creatures, however. They had a subdued, humble look, like dogs that are used to being kicked; very different from the bold free bearing of the men. The reason of this was, that they were treated by the men more as beasts of burden than companions. Women among the North American Indians have a hard time of it, poor creatures. While their lords and masters are out at the chase, or idly smoking round the fire, the Indian women are employed in cutting firewood and drawing water. Of course, they do all the cooking, and, as the eating always continues, so the cooking never stops. When these more severe labours are over, they employ their time in making and ornamenting coats, leggings, and moccasins — and very beautiful work they can turn out of their hands. On the voyage, the women use the paddle as well as the men, and, in journeying through the woods, they always carry or drag the heaviest loads. For all this they get few thanks, and often when the husbands become jealous, they get severely beaten and kicked.

It is always thus among savages; and it would seem that, just in proportion as men rise from the savage to the civilised state, they treat their women better. It is certain that when man embraces the blessed gospel of Christ and learns to follow the law of love, he places woman not only on a level with himself, but even above himself, and seeks her comfort and happiness before he seeks his own.

Few of the Red-men of North America are yet Christians, therefore they have no gallantry about them — no generous and chivalrous feelings towards the weaker sex. Most of their women are downtrodden and degraded.

The first night at Jasper's House was spent in smoking and talking. Here our friend Jasper Derry got news of Marie. To his immense delight he learned that she was well, and living with her father at Fort Erie, near the plains, or prairies as they are called, on the Saskatchewan River. A long journey still lay before our bold hunter, but that was nothing to him. He felt quite satisfied to hear that the girl of his heart was well, and still unmarried.

Next day the serious business of trading commenced at the outpost.

"I should like to get that powder and ball before you begin to trade with the Indians, Mr. Grant," said Jasper, after break-fast was concluded, "I'm anxious to be off as soon as possible."

"No, no, Jasper, I'll not give you a single charge of powder or an ounce of lead this day. You must spend another night with me, my man; I have not had half my talk out with you. You have no need to hurry, for Marie does not know you are coming, so of course she can't be impatient."

Mr. Grant said this with a laugh, for he knew the state of Jasper's heart, and understood why he was so anxious to hasten away.

"Besides," continued the fur-trader, "Mr. Heywood has not half finished the drawing of my fort, which he began yesterday, and I want him to make me a copy of it."

"I shall be delighted to do so," said the artist, who was busily engaged in arranging his brushes and colours.

"Well, well," cried Jasper. "I suppose I must submit. I fancy *you* have no objection to stop here another day, Arrowhead?"

The Indian nodded gravely, as he squatted down on the floor and began to fill his pipe.

"That's settled, then," said Jasper, "so I'll go with you to the store, if you'll allow me."

"With all my heart," replied the fur-trader, who forthwith led the way to the store, followed by the Indians with their packs of furs.

Now, the store or shop at a Hudson's Bay trading-post is a most interesting and curious place. To the Indian, especially, it is a sort of enchanted chamber, out of which can be obtained everything known under the sun. As there can be only one shop or store at a trading-post, it follows that that shop must contain a few articles out of almost every other style of shop in the world. Accordingly, you will find collected within the four walls of that little room, knives and guns from Sheffield, cotton webs from Manchester, grindstones from Newcastle, tobacco from Virginia, and every sort of thing from I know not where all! You can buy a blanket or a file, an axe or a pair of trousers, a pound of sugar or a barrel of nails, a roll of tobacco or a tin kettle, — everything, in short, that a man can think of or desire. And you can buy it, too, without money! Indeed, you *must* buy it without money, for there is not such a thing as money in the land.

The trade is carried on entirely by barter, or exchange. The Indian gives the trader his furs, and the trader gives him his goods. In order to make the exchange fair and equitable, however, everything is rated by a certain standard of value, which is called a *made-beaver* in one part of the country, a *castore* in another.

The first man that stepped forward to the counter was a chief. A big, coarse-looking, disagreeable man, but a first-rate hunter. He had two wives in consequence of his abilities, and the favourite wife now stood at his elbow to prompt, perhaps to caution, him. He threw down a huge pack of furs, which the trader opened, and examined with care, fixing the price of each skin, and marking it down with a piece of chalk on the counter as he went along.

There were two splendid black bear-skins, two or three dozen martens, or sables, five or six black foxes, and a great many silver foxes, besides cross and red ones. In addition to these, he had a number of minks and beaver-skins, a few otters, and sundry other furs, besides a few buffalo and deer-skins, dressed, and with the hair scraped off. These last skins are used for making winter coats, and also moccasins for the feet.

After all had been examined and valued, the whole was summed up, and a number of pieces of stick were handed to the chief — each stick representing a castore; so that he knew exactly how much he was worth, and proceeded to choose accordingly.

First he gazed earnestly at a huge thick blanket, then he counted his sticks, and considered. Perhaps the memory of the cold blasts of winter crossed his mind, for he quickly asked how many castores it was worth. The trader told him. The proper number of pieces of stick were laid down, and the blanket was handed over. Next a gun attracted his eye. The guns sent out for the Indian trade are very cheap ones, with blue barrels and red stocks. They shoot pretty well, but are rather apt to burst. Indeed this fate had befallen the chief's last gun, so he resolved to have another, and bought it. Then he looked earnestly for some time at a tin kettle. Boiled meat was evidently in his mind; but at this point his squaw plucked him by the sleeve. She whispered in his ear. A touch of generosity seemed to come over him, for he pointed to a web of bright scarlet cloth. A yard of this was measured off, and handed to his spouse, whose happiness for the moment was complete — for squaws in Rupert's Land, like the fair sex in England, are uncommonly fond of finery.

As the chief proceeded, he became more cautious and slow in his choice. Finery tempted him on the one hand, necessaries pressed him on the other, and at this point the trader stepped in to help him to decide; he recommended, warned, and advised. Twine was to be got for nets and fishing-lines, powder and shot, axes for cutting his winter firewood, cloth for his own and his wife's leggings, knives, tobacco, needles, and an endless variety of things, which gradually lessened his little pile of sticks, until at last he reached the sticking point, when all his sticks were gone.

"Now, Darkeye," (that was the chief's name), "you've come to the end at last, and a good thing you have made of it this year," said Mr. Grant, in the Indian language. "Have you got all you want?"

"Darkeye wants bullets," said the chief.

"Ah, to be sure. You shall have a lot of these for nothing, and some tobacco too," said the trader, handing the gifts to the Indian.

A look of satisfaction lighted up the chief's countenance

as he received the gifts, and made way for another Indian to open and display his pack of furs. But Jasper was struck by a peculiar expression in the face of Darkeye. Observing that he took up one of the bullets and showed it to another savage, our hunter edged near him to overhear the conversation.

"Do you see that ball?" said the chief, in a low tone.

The Indian to whom he spoke nodded.

"Look here!"

Darkeye put the bullet into his mouth as he spoke, and bit it until his strong sharp teeth sank deep into the lead; then, holding it up, he said, in the same low voice, "You will know it again?"

Once more the savage nodded, and a malicious smile played on his face for a moment.

Just then Mr. Grant called out, "Come here, Jasper, tell me what you think this otter-skin is worth."

Jasper's curiosity had been aroused by the mysterious conduct of Darkeye, and he would have given a good deal to have heard a little more of his conversation; but, being thus called away, he was obliged to leave his place, and soon forgot the incident.

During the whole of that day the trading of furs was carried on much as I have now described it. Some of the Indians had large packs, and some had small, but all of them had sufficient to purchase such things as were necessary for themselves and their families during the approaching winter; and as each man received from Mr. Grant a present of tobacco, besides a few trinkets of small value, they returned to the Hall that night in high good humour.

Next day, Jasper and his friends bade the hospitable trader farewell, and a few days after that the Indians left him. They smoked a farewell pipe, then struck their tents, and placed them and their packs of goods in the canoes, with their wives, children, and dogs. Pushing out into the stream, they commenced the return journey to their distant hunting-grounds. Once more their shouts rang through the forest, and rolled over the water, and once more the paddles sent the sparkling drops into the air as they dashed ahead, round the point of rocks above the fort, and disappeared; leaving the fur-trader, as they found him, smoking his pipe, with his hands in his pockets, and leaning against the door-post of his once-again silent and solitary home.

CHAPTER VII.

A Savage Family, and a Fight with a Bear.

About a week after our travellers left the outpost, Arrowhead had an adventure with a bear, which had well-nigh cut short his journey through this world, as well as his journey in the wilderness of Rupert's Land.

It was in the evening of a beautiful day when it happened. The canoe had got among some bad rapids, and, as it advanced very slowly, young Heywood asked to be put on shore, that he might walk up the banks of the river, which were very beautiful, and sketch.

In half an hour he was far ahead of the canoe. Suddenly, on turning round a rocky point, he found himself face to face with a small Indian boy. It is probable that the little fellow had never seen a white man before, and it is certain that Heywood had never seen such a specimen of a brown boy. He was clothed in skin, it is true, but it was the skin in which he had been born, for he had not a stitch of clothing on his fat little body.

As the man and the boy stood staring at each other, it would have been difficult to say which opened his eyes widest with amazement. At first Heywood fancied the urchin was a wild beast of some sort on two legs, but a second glance convinced him that he was a real boy. The next thought that occurred to the artist was, that he would try to sketch him, so he clapped his hand to his pocket, pulled out his book and pencil, and forthwith began to draw.

This terrified the little fellow so much, that he turned about and fled howling into the woods. Heywood thought of giving chase, but a noise attracted his attention at that moment, and, looking across the river, he beheld the boy's father in the same cool dress as his son. The man had been fishing, but when he saw that strangers were passing, he threw his blanket round him, jumped into his canoe, and crossed over to meet them.

This turned out to be a miserably poor family of Indians, consisting of the father, mother, three girls, and a boy, and a few ill-looking dogs. They all lived together in a little tent or wigwam, made partly of skins and partly of birch-bark. This tent was shaped like a cone. The fire was kindled inside, in the middle of the floor. A hole in the side served for a door, and a hole in the top did duty for window and chimney. The family kettle hung above the fire, and the family circle sat around it. A dirtier family and filthier tent one could not wish to see. The father was a poor weakly man and a bad hunter; the squaw was thin, wrinkled, and very dirty, and the children were all sickly-looking, except the boy before mentioned, who seemed to enjoy more than his fair share of health and rotundity.

"Have ye got anything to eat?" inquired Jasper, when the canoe reached the place.

They had not got much, only a few fish and an owl.

"Poor miserable critters," said Jasper, throwing them a goose and a lump of venison; "see there — that'll keep the wolf out o' yer insides for some time. Have ye got anything to smoke?"

No, they had nothing to smoke but a few dried leaves.

"Worse and worse," cried Jasper, pulling a large plug of tobacco from the breast of his coat; "here, that'll keep you puffin' for a short bit, anyhow."

Heywood, although no smoker himself, carried a small supply of tobacco just to give away to Indians, so he added two or three plugs to Jasper's gift, and Arrowhead gave the father a few charges of powder and shot. They then stepped into their canoe, and pushed off with that feeling of light hearted happiness which always follows the doing of a kind action.

"There's bears up the river," said the Indian, as they were leaving.

"Have ye seen them?" inquired Jasper.

"Ay, but could not shoot — no powder, no ball. Look out for them!"

"That will I," replied the hunter, and in another moment the canoe was out among the rapids again, advancing slowly up the river.

In about an hour afterwards they came to a part of the river where the banks were high and steep. Here Jasper landed to look for the tracks of the bears. He soon found these, and as they appeared to be fresh, he prepared to follow them up.

"We may as well encamp here," said he to Arrowhead; "you can go and look for the bears. I will land the baggage, and haul up the canoe, and then take my gun and follow you. I see that our friend Heywood is at work with his pencil already."

This was true. The keen artist was so delighted with the scene before him, that the moment the canoe touched the land he had jumped out, and, seating himself on the trunk of a fallen tree, with book and pencil, soon forgot everything that was going on around him.

Arrowhead shouldered his gun and went away up the river. Jasper soon finished what he had to do, and followed him, leaving Heywood seated on the fallen tree.

Now the position which Heywood occupied was rather dangerous. The tree lay on the edge of an overhanging bank of clay, about ten feet above the water, which was deep and rapid at that place. At first the young man sat down on the tree-trunk near its root, but after a time, finding the position not quite to his mind, he changed it, and went close to the edge of the bank. He was so much occupied with his drawing, that he did not observe that the ground on which his feet rested actually overhung the stream. As his weight rested on the fallen tree, however, he remained there safe enough and busy for half an hour.

At the end of that time he was disturbed by a noise in the bushes. Looking up, he beheld a large brown bear coming straight towards him. Evidently the bear did not see him, for it was coming slowly and lazily along, with a quiet meditative expression on its face. The appearance of the animal was so sudden and unexpected, that poor Heywood's heart almost leaped into his mouth. His face grew deadly pale, his long hair almost rose on his head with terror, and he was utterly unable to move hand or foot.

In another moment the bear was within three yards of him, and, being taken by surprise, it immediately rose on its hind legs, which is the custom of bears when about to make or receive an attack. It stared for a moment at the horrified artist.

Let not my reader think that Heywood's feelings were due to cowardice. The bravest of men have been panic-stricken when taken by surprise. The young man had never seen a bear before, except in a cage, and the difference between a caged and a free bear is very great. Besides, when a rough-looking monster of this kind comes unexpectedly on a man who is unarmed, and has no chance of escape, and rises on its hind legs, as if to let him have a full view of its enormous size, its great strength, and its ugly appearance, he may well be excused for feeling a little uncomfortable, and looking somewhat uneasy.

When the bear rose, as I have said, Heywood's courage returned. His first act was to fling his sketch-book in Bruin's face, and then, uttering a loud yell, he sprang to his feet, intending to run away. But the violence of his action broke off the earth under his feet. He dropt into the river like a lump of lead, and was whirled away in a moment!

What that bear thought when it saw the man vanish from the spot like a ghost, of course I cannot tell. It certainly *looked* surprised, and, if it was a bear of ordinary sensibility, it must undoubtedly have *felt* astonished. At any rate, after standing there, gazing for nearly a minute in mute amazement at the spot where Heywood had disappeared, it let itself down on its forelegs, and, turning round, walked slowly back into the bushes.

Poor Heywood could not swim, so the river did what it pleased with him. After sweeping him out into the middle of the stream, and rolling him over five or six times, and whirling him round in an eddy close to the land, and dragging him out again into the main current, and sending him struggling down a rapid, it threw him at last, like a bundle of old clothes, on a shallow, where he managed to get on his feet, and staggered to the shore in a most melancholy plight. Thereafter he returned to the encampment, like a drowned rat, with his long hair plastered to his thin face, and his soaked garments clinging tightly to his slender body. Had he been able to see himself at that moment, he would have laughed, but, not being able to see himself, and feeling very miserable, he sighed and shuddered with cold, and then set to work to kindle a fire and dry himself.

Meanwhile the bear continued its walk up the river. Arrowhead, after a time, lost the track of the bear he was in search of, and, believing that it was too late to follow it up farther that night, he turned about, and began to retrace his steps. Not long after that, he and the bear met face to face. Of course, the Indian's gun was levelled in an instant, but the meeting was so sudden, that the aim was not so true as usual, and, although the ball mortally wounded the animal, it did not kill him outright.

There was no time to re-load, so Arrowhead dropped his gun and ran. He doubled as he ran, and made for the encampment; but the bear ran faster. It was soon at the Indian's heels. Knowing that farther flight was useless, Arrowhead drew the hatchet that hung at his belt, and, turning round, faced the infuriated animal, which instantly rose on its hind legs and closed with him.

The Indian met it with a tremendous blow of his axe, seized it by the throat with his left hand, and endeavoured to repeat the blow. [See frontispiece.] But brave and powerful though he was, the Indian was like a mere child in the paw of the bear. The axe descended with a crash on the monster's head, and sank into its skull. But bears are notoriously hard to kill. This one scarcely seemed to feel the blow. Next instant Arrowhead was down, and, with its claws fixed in the man's back, the bear held him down, while it began to gnaw the fleshy part of his left shoulder.

No cry escaped from the prostrate hunter. He determined to lie perfectly still, as if he were dead, that being his only chance of escape; but the animal was furious, and there is little doubt that the Indian's brave spirit would soon have fled, had not God mercifully sent Jasper Derry to his relief.

That stout hunter had been near at hand when the shot was fired. He at once ran in the direction whence the sound came, and arrived on the scene of the struggle just as Arrowhead fell. Without a moment's hesitation he dropt on one knee, took a quick but careful aim and fired. The ball entered the bear's head just behind the ear and rolled it over dead!

Arrowhead's first act on rising was to seize the hand of his deliverer, and in a tone of deep feeling exclaimed, "My brother!"

"Ay," said Jasper with a quiet smile, as he reloaded his gun; "this is not the first time that you and I have helped one another in the nick of time, Arrowhead; we shall be brothers, and good friends to boot, I hope, as long as we live."

"Good," said the Indian, a smile lighting up for one moment his usually grave features.

"But my brother is wounded, let me see," said Jasper.

"It will soon be well," said the Indian carelessly, as he took off his coat and sat down on the bank, while the white hunter examined his wounds.

This was all that was said on the subject by these two men. They were used to danger in every form, and had often saved each other from sudden death. The Indian's wounds, though painful, were trifling. Jasper dressed them in silence, and then, drawing his long hunting knife, he skinned and cut up the bear, while his companion lay down on the bank, smoked his pipe, and looked on. Having cut off the best parts of the carcass for supper, the hunters returned to the canoe, carrying the skin along with them.

CHAPTER VIII.

Running the Falls — Wild Scenes and Men.

Next day the travellers reached one of those magnificent lakes of which there are so many in the wild woods of North America, and which are so like to the great ocean itself, that it is scarcely possible to believe them to be bodies of fresh water until they are tasted.

The largest of these inland seas is the famous Lake Superior, which is so enormous in size that ships can sail on its broad bosom for several days *out of sight* of land. It is upwards of three hundred miles long, and about one hundred and fifty broad. A good idea of its size may be formed from the fact, that it is large enough to contain the whole of Scotland, and deep enough to cover her highest hills!

The lake on which the canoe was now launched, although not so large as Superior, was, nevertheless, a respectable body of water, on which the sun was shining as if on a shield of bright silver. There were numbers of small islets scattered over its surface; some thickly wooded to the water's edge, others little better than bare rocks. Crossing this lake they came to the mouth of a pretty large stream and began to ascend it. The first thing they saw on rounding a bend in the stream was an

Indian tent, and in front of this tent was an Indian baby, hanging from the branch of a tree.

Let not the reader be horrified. The child was not hanging by the neck, but by the handle of its cradle, which its mother had placed there, to keep her little one out of the way of the dogs. The Indian cradle is a very simple contrivance. A young mother came out of the tent with her child just as the canoe arrived, and began to pack it in its cradle. Jasper stopped for a few minutes to converse with one of the Indians, so that the artist had a good opportunity of witnessing the whole operation.

The cradle was simply a piece of flat board, with a bit of scarlet cloth fastened down each side of it. First of all, the mother laid the poor infant, which was quite naked, sprawling on the ground. A dirty-looking dog took advantage of this to sneak forward and smell at it, whereupon the mother seized a heavy piece of wood, and hit the dog such a rap over the nose as sent it away howling. Then she spread a thick layer of soft moss on the wooden board. Above this she laid a very neat, small blanket, about two feet in length. Upon this she placed the baby, which objected at first to go to bed, squalled a good deal, and kicked a little. The mother therefore took it up, turned it over, gave it one or two hearty slaps, and laid it down again.

This seemed to quiet it, for it afterwards lay straight out, and perfectly still, with its coal-black eyes staring out of its fat brown face, as if it were astonished at receiving such rough treatment. The mother next spread a little moss over the child, and above that she placed another small blanket, which she folded and tucked in very comfortably, keeping the little one's arms close to its sides, and packing it all up, from neck to heels, so tightly that it looked more like the making up of a parcel than the wrapping up of a child. This done, she drew the scarlet cloth over it from each side of the cradle, and laced it down the front. When all was done, the infant looked like an Egyptian mummy, nothing but the head being visible.

The mother then leaned the cradle against the stem of a tree, and immediately one of the dogs ran against it, and knocked it over. Luckily, there was a wooden bar attached to the cradle, in front of the child's face, which bar is placed there on purpose to guard against injury from such accidents, so that the bar came first to the ground, and thus prevented the flattening of the child's nose, which, to say truth, was flat enough already!

Instead of scolding herself for her own carelessness, the Indian mother scolded the dog, and then hung the child on the branch of a tree, to keep it from further mischief.

The next turn in the river revealed a large waterfall, up which it was impossible to paddle, so they prepared to make a portage. Before arriving at the foot of it, however, Jasper landed Heywood, to enable him to make a sketch, and then the two men shoved off, and proceeded to the foot of the fall.

They were lying there in an eddy, considering where was the best spot to land, when a loud shout drew their attention towards the rushing water. Immediately after, a boat was seen to hover for a moment on the brink of the waterfall. This fall, although about ten or fifteen feet high, had such a large body of water rushing over it, that the river, instead of falling straight down, gushed over in a steep incline. Down this incline the boat now darted with the speed of lightning. It was full of men, two of whom stood erect, the one in the bow, the other in the stern, to control the movements of the boat.

For a few seconds there was deep silence. The men held their breath as the boat leaped along with the boiling flood.

There was a curling white wave at the foot of the fall. The boat cut through this like a knife, drenching her crew with spray. Next moment she swept round into the eddy where the canoe was floating, and the men gave vent to a loud cheer of satisfaction at having run the fall in safety.

But this was not the end of that exciting scene. Scarcely had they gained the land, when another boat appeared on the crest of the fall. Again a shout was given and a dash made. For one moment there was a struggle with the raging flood, and then a loud cheer as the second boat swept into the eddy in safety. Then a third and a fourth boat went through the same operation, and before the end of a quarter of an hour, six boats ran the fall. The bay at the foot of it, which had been so quiet and solitary when Jasper and his friends arrived, became the scene of the wildest confusion and noise, as the men ran about with tremendous activity, making preparations to spend the night there.

Some hauled might and main at the boats; some carried up the provisions, frying-pans, and kettles; others cut down dry trees with their axes, and cut them up into logs from five to six feet long, and as thick as a man's thigh. These were intended for six great fires, each boat's crew requiring a fire to themselves.

While this was going on, the principal guides and steersmen crowded round our three travellers, and plied them with questions; for it was so unusual to meet with strangers in that far-off wilderness, that a chance meeting of this kind was regarded as quite an important event.

"You're bound for York Fort, no doubt," said Jasper, addressing a tall handsome man of between forty and fifty, who was the principal guide.

"Ay, that's the end of our journey. You see we're taking our furs down to the coast. Have you come from York Fort, friend!"

"No, I've come all the way from Canada," said Jasper, who thereupon gave them a short account of his voyage.

"Well, Jasper, you'll spend the night with us, won't you?" said the guide.

"That will I, right gladly."

"Come, then, I see the fires are beginning to burn. We may as well have a pipe and a chat while supper is getting ready."

The night was now closing in, and the scene in the forest, when the camp-fires began to blaze, was one of the most stirring and romantic sights that could be witnessed in that land. The men of the brigade were some of them French-Canadians, some natives of the Orkney Islands, who had been hired and sent out there by the Hudson's Bay Company, others were half-breeds, and a few were pure Indians. They were all dressed in what is called *voyageur* costume-coats or capotes of blue or grey cloth, with hoods to come over their heads at night, and fastened round their waists with scarlet worsted belts; corduroy or grey trousers, gartered outside at the knees, moccasins, and caps. But most of them threw off their coats, and appeared in blue and red striped cotton shirts, which were open at the throat, exposing their broad, sun-burned, hairy chests. There was variety, too, in the caps — some had Scotch bonnets, others red nightcaps, a few had tall hats, ornamented with gold and silver cords and tassels, and a good many wore no covering at all except their own thickly-matted hair. Their faces were burned to every shade of red, brown, and black, from constant exposure, and they were strong as lions, wild as zebras, and frolicksome as kittens.

It was no wonder, then, that Heywood got into an extraordinary state of excitement and delight as he beheld these wild, fine-looking men smoking their pipes and cooking their suppers, sitting, lying, and standing, talking and singing, and laughing, with teeth glistening and eyes glittering in the red blaze of the fires — each of which fires was big enough to have roasted a whole ox!

The young artist certainly made good use of his opportunity. He went about from fire to fire, sketch-book in hand, sketching all the best-looking men in every possible attitude, sometimes singly, and sometimes in groups of five or six. He then went to the farthest end of the encampment, and, in the light of the last fire, made a picture of all the rest.

The kettles were soon steaming. These hung from tripods erected over the fires. Their contents were flour and pemmican, made into a thick soup called Rubbiboo.

As pemmican is a kind of food but little known in this country, I may as well describe how it is made. In the first place, it consists of buffalo meat. The great plains, or prairies, of America, which are like huge downs or commons hundreds of miles in extent, afford grass sufficient to support countless herds of deer, wild horses, and bisons. The bisons are called by the people there buffaloes. The buffalo is somewhat like an enormous ox, but its hind-quarters are smaller and its fore-quarters much larger than those of the ox. Its hair is long and shaggy, particularly about the neck and shoulders, where it becomes almost a mane. Its horns are thick and short, and its look is very ferocious, but it is in reality a timid creature, and will only turn to attack a man when it is hard pressed and cannot escape. Its flesh is first-rate for food, even better than beef, and there is a large hump on its shoulder, which is considered the best part of the animal.

Such is the bison, or buffalo, from which pemmican is made.

When a man wishes to make a bag of pemmican, he first of all kills the buffalo – not an easy thing to do by any means, for the buffalo runs well. Having killed him, he skins him and cuts up the meat – also a difficult thing to do, especially if one is not used to that sort of work. Then he cuts the meat into thin layers, and hangs it up to dry. Dried meat will keep for a long time. It is packed up in bales and sent about that country to be used as food. The next thing to be done is to make a bag of the raw hide of the buffalo. This is done with a glover's needle, the raw sinews of the animal being used instead of thread. The bag is usually about three feet long, and eighteen inches broad, and the hair is left on the outside of it. A huge pot is now put on the fire, and the fat of the buffalo is melted down. Then the dried meat is pounded between two stones, until it is torn and broken up into shreds, after which it is put into the bag, the melted fat is poured over it, and the whole is well mixed. The last operation is to sew up the mouth of the bag and leave it to cool, after which the pemmican is ready for use.

In this state a bag of pemmican will keep fresh and good for years. When the search was going on in the polar regions for the lost ships of Sir John Franklin, one of the parties hid some pemmican in the ground, intending to return and take it up. They returned home, however, another way. Five years later some travellers discovered this pemmican, and it was found, at that time, to be fit for food. Pemmican is extensively used throughout Rupert's Land, especially during summer, for at that season the brigades of boats start from hundreds of inland trading-posts to take the furs to the coast for shipment to England, and pemmican is found to be not only the best of food for these hard-working men, but exceedingly convenient to carry.

Supper finished, the wild-looking fellows of this brigade took to their pipes, and threw fresh logs on the fires, which roared, and crackled, and shot up their forked tongues of flame, as if they wished to devour the forest. Then the song and the story went round, and men told of terrible fights with the red-men of the prairies, and desperate encounters with grizzly bears in the Rocky Mountains, and narrow escapes among the rapids and falls, until the night was half spent. Then, one by one, each man wrapped himself in his blanket, stretched himself on the ground with his feet towards the fire and his head pillowed on a coat or a heap of brush-wood, and went to sleep.

Ere long they were all down, except one or two long-winded story tellers, who went on muttering to their pipes after their comrades were asleep. Even these became tired at last of the sound of their own voices, and gradually every noise in the camp was hushed, except the crackling of the fires as they sank by degrees and went out, leaving the place in dead silence and total darkness.

With the first peep of dawn the guide arose. In ten minutes after his first shout the whole camp was astir. The men yawned a good deal at first and grumbled a little, and stretched themselves violently, and yawned again. But soon they shook off laziness and sprang to their work. Pots, pans, kettles, and pemmican bags were tossed into the boats, and in the course of half-an-hour they were ready to continue the voyage.

Jasper stood beside the guide looking on at the busy scene.

"Heard you any news from the Saskatchewan of late," said he.

"Not much," replied the guide; "there's little stirring there just now, except among the Indians, who have been killing and scalping each other as usual. But, by the way, that reminds me there has been a sort of row between the Indians and the Company's people at Fort Erie."

"Fort Erie," said Jasper with a start.

"Ay, that's the name o' the fort, if I remember right," returned the guide. "It seems that one o' the men there, I think they call him Laroche — but what makes you start, friend Jasper? Do you know anything of this man."

"Yes, he's a friend of mine. Go on, let me hear about it."

"Well, there's not much to tell," resumed the guide. "This Laroche, it would appear, has got into hot water. He has a daughter, a good lookin' wench I'm told, and, better than that, a well-behaved one. One o' the Indians had been impertinent to the girl, so old Laroche, who seems to be a fiery fellow, up fist, hit him on the nose, and knocked the savage flat on his back. A tremendous howl was set up, and knives and hatchets were flourished; but Mr. Pemberton, who is in charge of Fort Erie, ran in and pacified them. The Indian that was floored vows he'll have the hair of old Laroche's head."

This taking the hair off people's heads, or scalping, as it is called, is a common practice among the North American Indians. When a savage kills his enemy he runs his scalping knife round the dead man's head, seizes the hair with his left hand and tears the scalp off. Indeed this dreadful cruelty is sometimes practised before death has occurred. The scalp with its lock of hair is taken home by the victor, and hung up in his tent as a trophy of war. The man who can show the greatest number of scalps is considered the greatest warrior. The dresses of Indian warriors are usually fringed with human scalp-locks.

"That's a bad business," said Jasper, who was concerned to hear such news of his intended father-in-law. "Do ye know the name o' this red-skinned rascal?"

"I heard it mentioned," said the guide, "but I can't remember it at this moment."

"The boats are ready to start," said one of the steersmen, coming up just then.

"Very good, let the men embark. Now, Jasper, we must part. Give us a shake o' your hand. A pleasant trip to you."

"The same to you, friend," said Jasper, returning the guide's squeeze.

In another minute the boats were away.

"Now, friends, we shall start," said Jasper, breaking the deep silence which followed the departure of the brigade.

"Good," said Arrowhead.

"I'm ready," said Heywood.

The canoe was soon in the water, and the men in their places; but they started that morning without a song. Arrowhead was never inclined to be noisy, Heywood was sleepy, and Jasper was rendered anxious by what he had heard of his friends at Fort Erie, so they paddled away in silence.

CHAPTER IX.

The Fort, and an Unexpected Meeting.

We turn now to a very different scene. It is a small fort or trading-post on the banks of a stream which flows through the prairie. The fort is very much like the one which has been already described, but somewhat stronger; and there are four block-houses or bastions, one at each corner, from which the muzzles of a few heavy guns may be seen protruding.

The trees and bushes have been cleared away from around this fort, and the strips of forest-land which run along both sides of the river are not so thickly wooded as the country through which the reader has hitherto been travelling. In front of the fort rolls the river. Immediately behind it lies the boundless prairie, which extends like a sea of grass, with scarcely a tree or bush upon it, as far as the eye can reach. This is Fort Erie.

You might ride for many days over that prairie without seeing anything of the forest, except a clump of trees and bushes here and there, and now and then a little pond. The whole region is extremely beautiful. One that ought to fill the hearts of men with admiration and love of the bountiful God who formed it. But men in those regions, at the time I write of, thought of little beauties of nature, and cared nothing for the goodness of God. At least this may be truly said of the red-skinned owners of the soil. It was otherwise with *some* of the white people who dwelt there.

Three weeks had passed away since the night spent by our friends with the brigade. It was now a beautiful evening, a little after sunset. The day's work at the fort had been finished, and the men were amusing themselves by racing their horses, of which fine animals there were great numbers at Fort Erie.

Just a little after the sun had gone down, three horsemen appeared on the distant prairie and came bounding at full gallop towards the fort. They were our friends Jasper, Heywood, and Arrowhead. These adventurous travellers had reached a fort farther down the river two days before, and, having been supplied with horses, had pushed forward by way of the plains.

On entering the belt of woods close to the fort, the horsemen reined in, and rode among the trees more cautiously.

"Here's the end of our journey at last," cried Jasper, on whose bronzed countenance there was a deep flush of excitement and a look of anxiety.

Just as he said this, Jasper's heart appeared to leap into his throat and almost choked him. Pulling up suddenly, he swallowed his heart, with some difficulty, and said —

"Hold on, lads. I'll ride round to the fort by way of the river, for reasons of my own. Push on, Heywood, with the Indian, and let Mr. Pemberton know I'm coming. See, I will give you the packet of letters we were asked to carry from the fort below. Now, make haste."

Heywood, though a little surprised at this speech, and at the manner of his friend, took the packet in silence and rode swiftly away, followed by the Indian. When they were gone, Jasper dismounted, tied his horse to a tree, and walked quickly into the woods in another direction.

Now this mysterious proceeding is not difficult to explain. Jasper had caught sight of a female figure walking under the trees at a considerable distance from the spot where he had pulled up. He knew that there were none but Indian women at Fort Erie at that time, and that, therefore, the only respectably dressed female at the place must needs be his own Marie Laroche. Overjoyed at the opportunity thus unexpectedly afforded him of meeting her alone, he hastened forward with a beating heart.

Marie was seated on the stump of a fallen tree when the hunter came up. She was a fair, beautiful woman of about five-and-twenty, with an air of modesty about her which attracted love, yet repelled familiarity. Many a good-looking and well-doing young fellow had attempted to gain the heart of Marie during the last two years, but without success – for this good reason, that her heart had been gained already.

She was somewhat startled when a man appeared thus suddenly before her. Jasper stood in silence for a few moments, with his arms crossed upon his breast, and gazed earnestly into her face.

As he did not speak, she said –

"You appear to be a stranger here. Have you arrived lately?"

Jasper was for a moment astonished that she did not at once recognise him, and yet he had no reason to be surprised. Besides the alteration that two years sometimes makes in a man, Jasper had made a considerable alteration on himself. When Marie last saw him, he had been in the habit of practising the foolish and unnatural custom of shaving; and he had carried it to such an extreme that he shaved off every-thing — whiskers, beard, and moustache. But within a year he had been induced by a wise friend to change his opinion on this subject. That friend had suggested, that as Providence had caused hair to grow on his cheeks, lips, and chin, it was intended to be worn, and that he had no more right to shave his face than a Chinaman had to shave his head. Jasper had been so far convinced, that he had suffered his whiskers to grow. These were now large and bushy, and had encroached so much on his chin as to have become almost a beard.

Besides this, not having shaved any part of his face during the last three weeks, there was little of it visible except his eyes, forehead, and cheek-bones. All the rest was more or less cov-ered with black hair.

No wonder, then, that Marie, who believed him to be two thousand miles away at that moment, did not recognise him in the increasing darkness of evening. The lover at once under-stood this, and he resolved to play the part of a stranger. He happened to have the power of changing his voice — a power possessed by many people — and, trusting to the increasing gloom to conceal him, and to the fact that he was the last person in the world whom Marie might expect to see there, he addressed her as follows: —

"I am indeed a stranger here; at least I have not been at the post for a very long time. I have just reached the end of a long voyage."

"Indeed," said the girl, interested by the stranger's grave manner. "May I ask where you have come from?"

"I have come all the way from Canada, young woman, and I count myself lucky in meeting with such a pleasant face at the end of my journey."

"From Canada!" exclaimed Marie, becoming still more

interested in the stranger, and blushing deeply as she asked —
"You have friends there, no doubt?"

"Ay, a few," said Jasper.

"And what has brought you such a long way into this wild wilderness?" asked Marie, sighing as she thought of the hundreds of miles that lay between Fort Erie and Canada.

"I have come here to get me a wife," replied Jasper.

"That is strange," said the girl, smiling, "for there are few but Indian women here. A stout hunter like you might find one nearer home, I should think."

Here Marie paused, for she felt that on such a subject she ought not to converse with a stranger. Yet she could not help adding, "But perhaps, as you say, you have been in this part of the world before, you may have some one in your mind?"

"I am engaged," said Jasper abruptly.

On hearing this Marie felt more at her ease, and, being of a very sympathetic nature, she at once courted the confidence of the stranger.

"May I venture to ask her name?" said Marie, with an arch smile.

"I may not tell," replied Jasper; "I have a comrade who is entitled to know this secret before any one else. Perhaps you may have heard of him, for he was up in these parts two years agone. His name is Jasper Derry."

The blood rushed to Marie's temples on hearing the name, and she turned her face away to conceal her agitation, while, in a low voice, she said —

"Is Jasper Derry, then, your intimate friend?"

"That is he — a very intimate friend indeed. But you appear to know him."

"Yes, I — I know him — I have seen him. I hope he is well," said Marie; and she listened with a beating heart for the answer, though she still turned her face away.

"Oh! he's well enough," said Jasper; "sickness don't often trouble *him*. He's going to be married."

Had a bullet struck the girl's heart she could not have turned more deadly pale than she did on hearing this. She half rose from the tree stump, and would have fallen to the ground insensible, had not Jasper caught her in his arms.

"My own Marie," said he fervently, "forgive me, dearest; forgive my folly, my wickedness, in deceiving you in this fashion. Oh, what a fool I am!" he added, as the poor girl still hung heavily in his grasp — "speak to me Marie, my own darling."

Whether it was the earnestness of his voice, or the kiss which he printed on her forehead, or the coolness of the evening air, I know not, but certain it is that Marie recovered in the course of a few minutes, and, on being convinced that Jasper really was her old lover, she resigned herself, wisely, to her fate, and held such an uncommonly long conversation with the bold hunter, that the moon was up and the stars were out before they turned their steps towards the Fort.

"Why, Jasper Derry," cried Mr. Pemberton, as the hunter entered the hall of Fort Erie, "where *have* you been. I've been expecting you every moment for the last two hours."

"Well, you see, Mr. Pemberton, I just went down the river a short bit to see an old friend and I was kep' longer than I expected," said Jasper, with a cool, grave face, as he grasped and shook the hand which was held out to him.

"Ah! I see, you hunters are more like brothers than friends. No doubt you went to smoke a pipe with Hawkeye, or to have a chat with the Muskrat about old times," said the fur-trader, mentioning the names of two Indians who were celebrated as being the best hunters in the neighbourhood, and who had been bosom friends of Jasper when he resided there two years before.

"No, I've not yet smoked a pipe with Hawkeye, neither have I seen Muskrat, but I certainly have had a pretty long chat with one o' my old friends," answered Jasper, while a quiet smile played on his face.

"Well, come along and have a pipe and a chat with *me*. I hope you count me one of your friends too," said Mr. Pemberton, conducting Jasper into an inner room, where he found Heywood and Arrowhead seated at a table, doing justice to a splendid supper of buffalo-tongues, venison-steaks, and marrow-bones.

"Here are your comrades, you see, hard at work. It's lucky you came to-night, Jasper, for I intend to be off to-morrow morning, by break of day, on a buffalo-hunt. If you had been a few hours later of arriving, I should have missed you. Come, will you eat or smoke?"

"I'll eat first, if you have no objection," said Jasper, "and smoke afterwards."

"Very good. Sit down, then, and get to work. Meanwhile I'll go and look after the horses that we intend to take with us to-morrow. Of course you'll accompany us, Jasper?"

"I'll be very glad, and so will Arrowhead, there. There's nothing he likes so much as a chase after a buffalo, unless, it may be, the eating of him. But as for my friend and comrade Mr. Heywood, he must speak for himself."

"I will be delighted to go," answered the artist, "nothing will give me more pleasure; but I fear my steed is too much exhausted to —"

"Oh! make your mind easy on that score," said the fur-trader, interrupting him. "I have plenty of capital horses, and can mount the whole of you, so that's settled. And now, friends, do justice to your supper, I shall be back before you have done."

So saying, Mr. Pemberton left the room, and our three friends, being unusually hungry, fell vigorously to work on the good cheer of Fort Erie.

CHAPTER X.

Buffalo-Hunting on the Prairies.

Next day most of the men of Fort Erie, headed by Mr. Pemberton, rode away into the prairies on a buffalo-hunt. Jasper would willingly have remained with Marie at the fort, but, having promised to go, he would not now draw back.

The band of horsemen rode for three hours, at a quick pace, over the grassy plains, without seeing anything. Jasper kept close beside his friend, old Laroche, while Heywood rode and conversed chiefly with Mr. Pemberton. There were about twenty men altogether, armed with guns, and mounted on their best buffalo-runners, as they styled the horses which were trained to hunt the buffalo. Many of these steeds had been wild horses, caught by the Indians, broken-in, and sold by them to the fur-traders.

"I have seldom ridden so long without meeting buffaloes," observed Mr. Pemberton, as the party galloped to the top of a ridge of land, from which they could see the plains far and wide around them.

"There they are at last," said Heywood eagerly, pointing to a certain spot on the far-off horizon where living creatures of some sort were seen moving.

"That must be a band o' red-skins," said Jasper, who trotted up at this moment with the rest of the party.

"They are Sauteaux," [This word is pronounced *Sotoes* in the plural; *Sotoe* in the singular] observed Arrowhead quietly.

"You must have good eyes, friend," said Pemberton, applying a small pocket-telescope to his eye; "they are indeed Sauteaux, I see by their dress, and they have observed us, for they are coming straight this way, like the wind."

"Will they come as enemies or friends?" inquired Heywood.

"As friends, I have no doubt," replied the fur-trader. "Come, lads, we will ride forward to meet them."

In a short time the two parties of horsemen met. They approached almost at full speed, as if each meant to ride the other down, and did not rein up until they were so close that it seemed impossible to avoid a shock.

"Have you seen the buffaloes lately?" inquired Pemberton, after the first salutation had passed.

"Yes, there are large bands not an hour's ride from this. Some of our young warriors have remained to hunt. We are going to the fort to trade."

"Good; you will find tobacco enough there to keep you smoking till I return with fresh meat," said Pemberton, in the native tongue, which he could speak like an Indian. "I'll not be long away. Farewell."

No more words were wasted. The traders galloped away over the prairie, and the Indians, of whom there were about fifteen, dashed off in the direction of the fort.

These Indians were a very different set of men from those whom I have already introduced to the reader in a former chapter. There are many tribes of Indians in the wilderness of Rupert's Land, and some of the tribes are at constant war with each other. But in order to avoid confusing the reader, it made be as well to divide the Indian race into two great classes — namely, those who inhabit the woods, and those who roam over the plains or prairies. As a general rule, the thick wood Indians are a more peaceful set of men than the prairie Indians. They are few in number, and live in a land full of game, where there is far more than enough of room for all of them. Their mode of travelling in canoes, and on foot, is slow, so that the different tribes do not often meet, and they have no occasion to quarrel. They are, for the most part, a quiet and harmless race of savages, and being very dependent on the fur-traders for the necessaries of life, they are on their good behaviour, and seldom do much mischief.

It is very different with the plain Indians. These savages have numbers of fine horses, and live in a splendid open country, which is well-stocked with deer and buffaloes, besides other game. They are bold riders, and scour over the country in all directions, consequently the different tribes often come across each other when out hunting. Quarrels and fights are the results, so that these savages are naturally a fierce and war-like race. They are independent too; for although they get their guns and ammunition and other necessaries from the traders, they can manage to live without these things if need be. They can clothe themselves in the skins of wild animals, and when they lose their guns, or wet their powder, they can kill game easily with their own bows and arrows.

It was a band of these fellows that now went galloping towards Fort Erie, with the long manes and tails of the half-wild horses and the scalp-locks on their dresses and their own long black hair streaming in the wind.

Pemberton and his party soon came up with the young Indians who had remained to chase the buffaloes. He found them sheltered behind a little mound, making preparations for an immediate attack on the animals, which, however, were not yet visible to the men from the fort.

"I do believe they've seen buffaloes on the other side of that mound," said Pemberton, as he rode forward.

He was right. The Indians, of whom there were six, well mounted and armed with strong short bows, pointed to the mound, and said that on the other side of it there were hundreds of buffaloes.

As the animals were so numerous, no objection was made to the fur-traders joining in the hunt, so in another moment the united party leaped from their horses and prepared for action. Some wiped out and carefully loaded their guns, others examined the priming of their pieces, and chipped the edges off the flints to make sure of their not missing fire. All looked to the girths of their saddles, and a few threw off their coats and rolled their shirt-sleeves up to their shoulders, as if they were going to undertake hard and bloody work.

Mr. Pemberton took in hand to look after our friend Heywood; the rest were well qualified to look after themselves. In five minutes they were all remounted and rode quietly to the brow of the mound.

Here an interesting sight presented itself. The whole plain was covered with the huge unwieldy forms of the buffaloes. They were scattered about, singly and in groups, grazing or playing or lying down, and in one or two places some of the bulls were engaged in single combat, pawing the earth, goring each other, and bellowing furiously.

After one look, the hunters dashed down the hill and were in the midst of the astonished animals almost before they could raise their heads to look at them. Now commenced a scene which it is not easy to describe correctly. Each man had selected his own group of animals, so that the whole party was scattered in a moment.

"Follow me," cried Pemberton to Heywood, "observe what I do, and then go try it yourself."

The fur-trader galloped at full speed towards a group of buffaloes which stood right before him, about two hundred yards off. He carried a single-barrelled gun with a flint lock in his right hand and a bullet in his mouth, ready to re-load. The buffaloes gazed at him for one moment in stupid surprise, and then, with a toss of their heads and a whisk of their tails, they turned and fled. At first they ran with a slow awkward gait, like pigs; and to one who did not know their powers, it would seem that the fast-running horses of the two men would quickly overtake them. But as they warmed to the work their speed increased, and it required the horses to get up their best paces to overtake them.

After a furious gallop, Pemberton's horse ran close up alongside of a fine-looking buffalo cow — so close that he could almost touch the side of the animal with the point of his gun. Dropping the rein, he pointed the gun without putting it to his shoulder and fired. The ball passed through the animal's heart, and it dropt like a stone. At the same moment Pemberton flung his cap on the ground beside it, so that he might afterwards claim it as his own.

The well-trained horse did not shy at the shot, neither did it check its pace for a moment, but ran straight on and soon placed its master alongside of another buffalo cow. In the meantime, Pemberton loaded like lightning. He let the reins hang loose, knowing that the horse understood his work, and, seizing the powder-horn at his side with his right hand, drew the wooden stopper with his teeth, and poured a charge of powder into his left — guessing the quantity, of course.

Pouring this into the gun he put the muzzle to his mouth, and spat the ball into it, struck the butt on the pommel of the saddle to send it down, as well as to drive the powder into the pan, and taking his chance of the gun priming itself, he aimed as before, and pulled the trigger. The explosion followed, and a second buffalo lay dead upon the plain, with a glove beside it to show to whom it belonged.

Scenes similar to this were being enacted all over the plain, with this difference, that the bad or impatient men sometimes fired too soon and missed their mark, or by only wounding the animals, infuriated them and caused them to run faster. One or two ill-trained horses shied when the guns were fired, and left their riders sprawling on the ground. Others stumbled into badger-holes and rolled over. The Indians did their work well. They were used to it, and did not bend their bows until their horses almost brushed the reeking sides of the huge brutes. Then they drew to the arrow heads, and, leaning forward, buried the shafts up to the feathers. The arrow is said to be even more deadly than the bullet.

Already the plain was strewn with dead or dying buffaloes, and the ground seemed to tremble with the thunder of the tread of the affrighted animals. Jasper had 'dropt' three, and Arrowhead had slain two, yet the pace did not slacken — still the work of death went on.

Having seen Pemberton shoot another animal, Heywood became fired with a desire to try his own hand, so he edged away from his companion. Seeing a very large monstrous-looking buffalo flying away by itself at no great distance, he turned his horse towards it, grasped his gun, shook the reins, and gave chase.

Now poor Heywood did not know that the animal he had made up his mind to kill was a tough old bull; neither did he know that a bull is bad to eat, and dangerous to follow; and, worse than all, he did not know that when a bull holds his tail stiff and straight up in the air, it is a sign that he is in a tremendous rage, and that the wisest thing a man can do is to let him alone. Heywood, in fact, knew nothing, so he rushed blindly on his fate. At first the bull did not raise his tail, but, as the rider drew near, he turned his enormous shaggy head a little to one side, and looked at him out of the corner of his wicked little eye. When Heywood came within a few yards and, in attempting to take aim, fired off his gun by accident straight into the face of the sun, the tail went up and the bull began to growl. The ferocious aspect of the creature alarmed the artist, but he had made up his mind to kill it, so he attempted to reload, as Pemberton had done. He succeeded, and, as he was about to turn his attention again to the bull, he observed one of the men belonging to the fort making towards him. This man saw and knew the artist's danger, and meant to warn him, but his horse unfortunately put one of its feet into a hole, and sent him flying head over heels through the air. Heywood was now so close to the bull that he had to prepare for another shot.

The horse he rode was a thoroughly good buffalo-runner. It knew the dangerous character of the bull, if its rider did not, and kept its eye watchfully upon it. At last the bull lost patience, and, suddenly wheeling round, dashed at the horse, but the trained animal sprang nimbly to one side, and got out of the way. Heywood was all but thrown. He clutched the mane, however, and held on. The bull then continued its flight.

Determined not to be caught in this way again, the artist seized the reins, and ran the horse close alongside of the buffalo, whose tail was now as stiff as a poker. Once more the bull turned suddenly round. Heywood pulled the reins violently, thus confusing his steed which ran straight against the buffalo's big hairy forehead. It was stopped as violently as if it had run against the side of a house. But poor Heywood was not stopped. He left the saddle like a rocket, flew right over the bull's back, came down on his face, ploughed up the land with his nose — and learned a lesson from experience!

Fortunately the spot on which he fell happened to be one of those soft muddy places in which the buffaloes are fond of rolling their huge bodies in the heat of summer, so that, with the exception of a bruised and dirty face, and badly soiled clothes, the bold artist was none the worse for his adventure.

CHAPTER XI.

Winter — Sleeping in the Snow — A Night Alarm.

Summer passed away, autumn passed away, and winter came. So did Christmas, and so did Jasper's marriage-day.

Now the reader must understand that there is a wonderful difference between the winter in that part of the North American wilderness called Rupert's land, and winter in our own happy island.

Winter out there is from six to eight months long. The snow varies from three to four feet deep, and in many places it drifts to fifteen or twenty feet deep. The ice on the lakes and rivers is sometimes above six feet thick; and the salt sea itself, in Hudson's Bay, is frozen over to a great extent. Nothing like a thaw takes place for many months at a time, and the frost is so intense that it is a matter of difficulty to prevent one's-self from being frost-bitten. The whole country, during these long winter months, appears white, desolate, and silent.

Yet a good many of the birds and animals keep moving about, though most of them do so at night, and do not often meet the eye of man. The bear goes to sleep all winter in a hole, but the wolf and the fox prowl about the woods at night. Ducks, geese, and plover no longer enliven the marshes with their wild cries; but white grouse, or ptarmigan, fly about in immense flocks, and arctic hares make many tracks in the deep snow. Still, these are quiet creatures, and they scarcely break the deep dead silence of the forests in winter.

At this period the Indian and the fur-trader wrap themselves in warm dresses of deer-skin, lined with the thickest flannel, and spend their short days in trapping and shooting. At night the Indian piles logs on his fire to keep out the frost, and adds to the warmth of his skin-tent by heaping snow up the outside of it all round. The fur-trader puts double window-frames and double panes of glass in his windows, puts on double doors, and heats his rooms with cast-iron stoves.

But do what he will, the fur-trader cannot keep out the cold altogether. He may heat the stove red-hot if he will, yet the water in the basins and jugs in the corner of his room will be frozen, and his breath settles on the window-panes, and freezes there so thickly that it actually dims the light of the sun. This crust on the windows *inside* is sometimes an inch thick!

Thermometers in England are usually filled with quicksilver. In Rupert's Land quicksilver would be frozen half the winter, so spirit of wine is used instead, because that liquid will not freeze with any ordinary degree of cold. Here, the thermometer sometimes falls as low as zero. Out there it does not rise so high as zero during the greater part of the winter, and it is often as low as twenty, thirty, and even fifty degrees *below* zero.

If the wind should blow when the cold is intense, no man dare face it — he would be certain to be frost-bitten. The parts of the body that are most easily frozen are the ears, the chin, the cheek-bones, the nose, the heels, fingers, and toes. The freezing of any part begins with a pricking sensation. When this occurs at the point of your nose, it is time to give earnest attention to that feature, else you run the risk of having it shortened. The best way to recover it is to rub it well, and to keep carefully away from the fire.

The likest thing to a frost-bite is a burn. In fact, the two things are almost the same. In both cases the skin or flesh is destroyed, and becomes a sore. In the one case it is destroyed by fire, in the other by frost; but in both it is painful and dangerous, according to the depth of the frost-bite or the burn. Many a poor fellow loses joints of his toes and fingers — some have even lost their hands and feet by frost. Many have lost their lives. But the most common loss is the loss of the skin of the point of the nose, cheek-bones, and chin — a loss which is indeed painful, but can be replaced by nature in the course of time.

Of course curious appearances are produced by such intense cold. On going out into the open air, the breath settles on the breast, whiskers, and eyebrows in the shape of hoar-frost; and men who go out in the morning for a ramble with black or brown locks, return at night with what appears to be grey hair — sometimes with icicles hanging about their faces. Horses and cattle there are seldom without icicles hanging from their lips and noses in winter.

Poor Mr. Pemberton was much troubled in this way. He was a fat and heavy man, and apt to perspire freely. When he went out to shoot in winter, the moisture trickled down his face and turned his whiskers into two little blocks of ice; and he used to be often seen, after a hard day's walk, sitting for a long time beside the stove, holding his cheeks to the fire, and gently coaxing the icy blocks to let go their hold!

But for all this, the long winter of those regions is a bright enjoyable season. The cold is not felt so much as one would expect, because it is not *damp*, and the weather is usually bright and sunny.

From what I have said, the reader will understand that summer in those regions is short and very hot; the winter long and very cold. Both seasons have their own peculiar enjoyments, and, to healthy men, both are extremely agreeable.

I have said that Jasper's marriage-day had arrived. New Year's Day was fixed for his union with the fair and gentle Marie. As is usual at this festive season of the year, it was arranged that a ball should be given at the fort in the large hall to all the people that chanced to be there at the time.

Old Laroche had been sent to a small hut a long day's march from the fort, where he was wont to spend his time in trapping foxes. He was there alone, so, three days before New Year's Day, Jasper set out with Arrowhead to visit the old man, and bear him company on his march back to the fort.

There are no roads in that country. Travellers have to plod through the wilderness as they best can. It may not have occurred to my reader that it would be a difficult thing to walk for a day through snow so deep, that, at every step, the traveller would sink the whole length of his leg. The truth is, that travelling in Rupert's Land in winter would be impossible but for a machine which enables men to walk on the surface of the snow without sinking more than a few inches. This machine is the snowshoe. Snow-shoes vary in size and form in different parts of the country, but they are all used for the same purpose. Some are long and narrow; others are nearly round. They vary in size from three to six feet in length, and from eight to twenty inches in breadth. They are extremely light — made of a frame-work of hard wood, and covered with a network of deer-skin, which, while it prevents the wearer from sinking more than a few inches, allows any snow that may chance to fall on the top of the shoe to pass through the netting.

The value of this clumsy looking machine may be imagined, when I say that men with them will easily walk twenty, thirty, and even forty miles across a country over which they could not walk three miles without such helps.

It was a bright, calm, frosty morning when Jasper and his friend set out on their short journey. The sun shone brilliantly, and the hoar-frost sparkled on the trees and bushes, causing them to appear as if they had been covered with millions of diamonds. The breath of the two men came from their mouths like clouds of steam. Arrowhead wore the round snow-shoes which go by the name of bear's paws — he preferred these to any others. Jasper wore the snow-shoes peculiar to the Chipewyan Indians. They were nearly as long as himself, and turned up at the point. Both men were dressed alike, in the yellow leathern costume of winter. The only difference being that Jasper wore a fur cap, while Arrowhead sported a cloth head-piece that covered his neck and shoulders, and was ornamented with a pair of horns.

All day the two men plodded steadily over the country. Sometimes they were toiling through deep snow in wooded places, sinking six or eight inches in spite of their snow-shoes. At other times they were passing swiftly over the surface of the open plains, where the snow was beaten so hard by exposure to the sun and wind that the shoes only just broke the crust and left their outlines behind.

Then they reached a bend of the river, where they had again to plod heavily through the woods on its banks, until they came out upon its frozen surface. Here the snow was so hard, that they took off their snow-shoes and ran briskly along without them for a long space.

Thus they travelled all day, without one halt, and made

such good use of their time, that they arrived at the log-hut of old Laroche early in the evening.

"Well met, son-in-law, *that is to be*," cried the stout old man heartily, as the two hunters made their appearance before the low door-way of his hut, which was surrounded by trees and almost buried in snow. "If you had been half an hour later, I would have met you in the woods."

"How so, father-in-law, *that is to be*," said Jasper, "were ye goin' out to your traps so late as this?"

"Nay, man, but I was startin' for the fort. It's a long way, as you know, and my old limbs are not just so supple as yours. I thought I would travel to-night, and sleep in the woods, so as to be there in good time to-morrow. But come in, come in, and rest you. I warrant me you'll not feel inclined for more walkin' to-night."

"Now my name is not Jasper Derry if I enter your hut this night," said the hunter stoutly. "If I could not turn round and walk straight back to the fort this night, I would not be worthy of your daughter, old man. So come along with you. What say you, Arrowhead; shall we go straight back?"

"Good," answered the Indian.

"Well, well," cried Laroche, laughing, "lead the way, and I will follow in your footsteps. It becomes young men to beat the track, and old ones to take it easy."

The three men turned their faces towards Fort Erie, and were soon far away from the log-hut. They walked steadily and silently along, without once halting, until the night became so dark that it was difficult to avoid stumps and bushes. Then they prepared to encamp in the snow.

Now it may seem to many people a very disagreeable idea, that of sleeping out in snow, but one who has tried it can assure them that it is not so bad as it seems. No doubt, when

Jasper halted in the cold dark woods, and said, "I think this will be a pretty good place to sleep," any one unacquainted with the customs of that country would have thought the man was jesting or mad; for, besides being very dismal, in consequence of its being pitch dark, it was excessively cold, and snow was falling steadily and softly on the ground. But Jasper knew what he was about, and so did the others. Without saying a word, the three men flung down their bundles of provisions, and each set to work to make the encampment. Of course they had to work in darkness so thick that even the white snow could scarcely be seen.

First of all they selected a tree, the branches of which were so thick and spreading as to form a good shelter from the falling snow. Here Jasper and Laroche used their snow-shoes as shovels, while Arrowhead plied his axe and soon cut enough of firewood for the night. He also cut a large bundle of small branches for bedding. A space of about twelve feet long, by six broad, was cleared at the foot of the tree in half an hour. But the snow was so deep that they had to dig down four feet before they reached the turf. As the snow taken out of the hole was thrown up all round it, the walls rose to nearly seven feet.

Arrowhead next lighted a roaring fire at one end of this cleared space, the others strewed the branches over the space in front of it, and spread their blankets on the top, after which the kettle was put on to boil, buffalo steaks were stuck up before the fire to roast, and the men then lay down to rest and smoke, while supper was preparing. The intense cold prevented the fire from melting the snowy walls of this encampment, which shone and sparkled in the red blaze like pink marble studded all over with diamonds, while the spreading branches formed a ruddy-looking ceiling. When they had finished supper, the heat of the fire and the heat of their food made the travellers feel quite warm and comfortable, in spite of John Frost; and when they at last wrapped their blankets round them and laid their heads together on the branches, they fell into a sleep more sound and refreshing than they would have enjoyed had they gone to rest in a warm house upon the best bed in England.

But when the fire went out, about the middle of the night, the cold became so intense that they were awakened by it, so Jasper rose and blew up the fire, and the other two sat up and filled their pipes, while their teeth chattered in their heads. Soon the blaze and the smoke warmed them, and again they lay down to sleep comfortably till morning.

Before daybreak, however, Arrowhead — who never slept so soundly but that he could be wakened by the slightest unusual noise — slowly raised his head and touched Jasper on the shoulder. The hunter was too well-trained to the dangers of the wilderness to start up or speak. He uttered no word but took up his gun softly and looked in the direction in which the Indian's eyes gazed. A small red spot in the ashes served to reveal a pair of glaring eye-balls among the bushes.

"A wolf," whispered Jasper, cocking his gun. "No; a man," said Arrowhead.

At the sound of the click of the lock the object in the bushes moved. Jasper leaped up in an instant, pointed his gun, and shouted sternly —

"Stand fast and speak, or I fire!"

At the same moment Arrowhead kicked the logs of the fire, and a bright flame leapt up, showing that the owner of the pair of eyes was an Indian. Seeing that he was discovered, and that if he turned to run he would certainly be shot, the savage came forward sulkily and sat down beside the fire. Jasper asked him why he came there in that stealthy manner like a sly fox.

The Indian said he was merely travelling by night, and had come on the camp unexpectedly. Not knowing who was there, he had come forward with caution.

Jasper was not satisfied with this reply. He did not like the look of the man, and he felt sure that he had seen him somewhere before, but his face was disfigured with war paint, and he could not feel certain on that point until he remembered the scene in the trading store at Jasper's House.

"What — Darkeye!" cried he, "can it be you?"

"Darkeye!" shouted Laroche, suddenly rising from his reclining position and staring the Indian in the face with a dark scowl. "Why, Jasper, this is the villain who insulted my daughter, and to whom I taught the lesson that an old man could knock him down."

The surprise and indignation of Jasper on hearing this was great, but remembering that the savage had already been punished for his offence, and that it would be mean to take advantage of him when there were three to one, he merely said —

"Well, well, I won't bear a grudge against a man who is coward enough to insult a woman. I would kick you out o' the camp, Darkeye, but as you might use your gun when you got into the bushes, I won't give you that chance. At the same time, we can't afford to lose the rest of our nap for you, so Arrowhead will keep you safe here and watch you, while Laroche and I sleep. We will let you go at daybreak."

Saying this Jasper lay down beside his father-in-law, and they were both asleep in a few minutes, leaving the two Indians to sit and scowl at each other beside the fire.

CHAPTER XII.

The Wedding, an Arrival, a Feast, and a Ball.

New Year's Day came at last, and on the morning of that day Jasper Derry and Marie Laroche were made man and wife. They were married by the Reverend Mr. Wilson, a Wesleyan missionary, who had come to Fort Erie, a few days before, on a visit to the tribes of Indians in that neighbourhood.

The North American Indian has no religion worthy of the name; but he has a conscience, like other men, which tells him that it is wrong to murder and to steal. Yet, although he knows this, he seldom hesitates to do both when he is tempted thereto. Mr. Wilson was one of those earnest missionaries who go to that wilderness and face its dangers, as well as its hardships and sufferings, for the sake of teaching the savage that the mere knowledge of right and wrong is not enough — that the love of God, wrought in the heart of man by the Holy Spirit, alone can enable him to resist evil and do good — that belief in the Lord Jesus Christ alone can save the soul.

There are several missionaries of this stamp — men who love the name of Jesus — in that region, and there are a number of stations where the good seed of God's Word is being planted in the wilderness. But I have not space, and this is not the place, to enlarge on the great and interesting subject of missionary work in Rupert's Land. I must return to my narrative.

It was, as I have said, New Year's day when Jasper and Marie were married. And a remarkably bright, beautiful morning it was. The snow appeared whiter than usual, and the countless gems of hoar-frost that hung on shrub and tree seemed to sparkle more than usual; even the sun appeared to shine more brightly than ever it did before — at least it seemed so in the eyes of Jasper and Marie.

"Everything seems to smile on us to-day, Marie," said Jasper, as they stood with some of their friends at the gate of the fort, just after the ceremony was concluded.

"I trust that God may smile on you, and bless your union, my friends," said Mr. Wilson, coming forward with a small Bible in his hand. "Here is a copy of God's Word, Jasper, which I wish you to accept of and keep as a remembrance of me and of this day."

"I'll keep it, sir, and I thank you heartily," said Jasper, taking the book and returning the grasp of the missionary's hand.

"And my chief object in giving it to you, Jasper, is, that you and Marie may read it often, and find joy and peace to your souls."

As the missionary said this a faint sound, like the tinkling of distant bells, was heard in the frosty air.

Looks of surprise and excitement showed that this was an unwonted sound. And so it was; for only once or twice during the long winter did a visitor gladden Fort Erie with his presence. These sweet sounds were the tinkling of sleigh-bells, and they told that a stranger was approaching — that letters, perhaps, and news from far-distant homes, might be near at band.

Only twice in the year did the Europeans at that lonely

outpost receive letters from home. Little wonder that they longed for them, and that they went almost wild with joy when they came.

Soon the sleigh appeared in sight, coming up the river at full speed, and a loud "hurrah!" from the men at the gate, told the visitor that he was a welcome guest. It was a dog-sleigh — a sort of conveyance much used by the fur-traders in winter travelling. In form, it was as like as possible to a tin slipper bath. It might also be compared to a shoe. If the reader will try to conceive of a shoe large enough to hold a man, sitting with his legs out before him, that will give him a good idea of the shape of a dog cariole. There is sometimes an ornamental curve in front. It is made of two thin hardwood planks curled up in front, with a light frame-work of wood, covered over with deer or buffalo skin, and painted in a very gay manner. Four dogs are usually harnessed to it, and these are quite sufficient to drag a man on a journey of many days, over every sort of country, where there is no road whatever. Dogs are much used for hauling little sledges in that country in winter. The traveller sits wrapped up so completely in furs, that nothing but his head is visible. He is attended by a driver on snow-shoes, who is armed with a large whip. No reins are used. If the snow is hard, as is usually the case on the surface of a lake or river, the driver walks behind and holds on to a tail-line, to prevent the dogs from running away. If the traveller's way lies through the woods, the snow is so soft and deep that the poor dogs are neither willing nor able to run away. It is as much as they can do to walk; so the driver goes before them, in this case, and beats down the snow with his snow-shoes — "beats the track," as it is called. The harness of the dogs is usually very gay, and covered with little bells which give forth a cheerful tinkling sound.

"It's young Cameron," cried Mr. Pemberton, hastening

forward to welcome the newcomer.

Cameron was the gentleman in charge of the nearest out-post — two hundred and fifty miles down the river.

"Welcome, Cameron, my boy, welcome to Fort Erie. You are the pleasantest sight we have seen here for many a day," said Pemberton, shaking the young man heartily by the hand as soon as he had jumped out of his sleigh.

"Come, Pemberton, you forget Miss Marie Laroche when you talk of my being the pleasantest sight," said Cameron, laughing.

"Ah! true. Pardon me, Marie —"

"Excuse me, gentlemen," interrupted Jasper, with much gravity, "I know of no such person as Miss Marie Laroche!"

"How? what do you mean?" said Cameron, with a puzzled look.

"Jasper is right," explained Pemberton, "Marie was *Miss Laroche* yesterday; she is *Mrs. Derry* to-day."

"Then I salute you, Mrs. Derry, and congratulate you both," cried the young man, kissing the bride's fair cheek, "and I rejoice to find that I am still in time to dance at your wedding."

"Ay," said Pemberton, as they moved up to the hall, "that reminds me to ask you why you are so late. I expected you before Christmas Day."

"I had intended to be here by that day," replied Cameron, "but one of my men cut his foot badly with an axe, and I could not leave him; then my dogs broke down on the journey, and that detained me still longer. But you will forgive my being so late, I think, when I tell you that I have got a packet of letters with me."

"Letters!" shouted every one.

"Ay, letters and newspapers from England."

A loud cheer greeted this announcement. The packet was hauled out of the sleigh, hurried up to the fort, torn open with eager haste, and the fur-traders of Fort Erie were soon devouring the contents like hungry men.

And they *were* hungry men — they were starving! Those who see their kindred and friends daily, or hear from them weekly, cannot understand the feelings of men who hear from them only twice in the year. Great improvements have taken place in this matter of late years; still, many of the Hudson Bay Company's outposts are so distant from the civilised world, that they cannot get news from "home" oftener than twice a year.

It was a sight to study and moralise over — the countenances of these banished men. The trembling anxiety lest there should be "bad news." The gleam of joy, and the deep "thank God," on reading "all well." Then the smiles, the sighs, the laughs, the exclamations of surprise, perhaps the tears that *would* spring to their eyes as they read the brief but, to them, thrilling private history of the past half year.

There was no bad news in that packet, and a feeling of deep joy was poured into the hearts of the people of the fort by these "Good news from a far country." Even the half-breeds and Indians, who could not share the feeling, felt the sweet influence of the general happiness that was diffused among the fur-traders on that bright New Year's Day in the wilderness.

What a dinner they had that day to be sure! What juicy roasts of buffalo beef; what enormous steaks of the same; what a magnificent venison pasty; and what glorious marrow-bones — not to mention tongues, and hearts, and grouse, and other things! But the great feature of the feast was the plum-pudding. It was like a huge cannon-ball with the measles! There was wine, too, on this occasion. Not much, it is true, but more than enough, for it had been saved up all the year expressly for the Christmas and New Year's festivities. Thus they were enabled to drink to absent friends, and bring up all the old toasts and songs that used to be so familiar long ago in the "old country." But these sturdy traders needed no stimulants. There were one or two who even scorned the wine, and stuck to water, and to their credit be it said, that they toasted and sang with the best of them.

At night there was a ball, and the ball beat the dinner out of sight. Few indeed were the women, but numerous were the men. Indian women are not famous for grace or cleanliness, poor things. But they enjoyed the ball, and they did their best to dance. Such dancing! They seemed to have no joints. They stood up stiff as lamp-posts, and went with an up-and-down motion from side to side. But the men did the thing bravely, especially the Indians. The only dances attempted were Scotch reels, and the Indians tried to copy the fur-traders; but on finding this somewhat difficult, they introduced some surprising steps of their own, which threw the others entirely into the shade! There was unfortunately no fiddler, but there was a fiddle — one made of pine wood by an Indian, with strings of deer-skin sinew. Some of the boldest of the party scraped *time* without regard to *tune*, and our friend Heywood beat the kettle-drum. The tones of the fiddle at last became so horrible that it was banished altogether, and they danced that night to the kettle-drum!

Of course the fair bride was the queen of that ball. Her countenance was the light of it, and her modest, womanly manner had a softening influence on the rough men who surrounded her.

When the ball was over, a curious thing occurred in the hall in which it had taken place. The room was heated by a stove, and as a stove dries the air of a room too much, it was customary to keep a pan of water on the stove to moisten it a little. This moisture was increased that night by the steam of the supper and by the wild dancing, so that, when all was over, the walls and ceiling were covered with drops of water. During the night this all froze in the form of small beautifully-shaped crystals, and in the morning they found themselves in a crystal palace of nature's own formation, which beat all the crystal palaces that ever were heard of — at least in originality, if not in splendour.

Thus happily ended the marriage-day of honest Jasper Derry and sweet Marie Laroche, and thus pleasantly began the new year of 18 — . But as surely as darkness follows light, and night follows day, so surely does sorrow tread on the heels of joy in the history of man. God has so ordained it, and he is wise who counts upon experiencing both.

CHAPTER XIII.

The Conclusion.

A week after the events narrated in the last chapter, Jasper Derry was sitting beside the stove in the hall at Fort Erie, smoking his pipe and conversing with his father-in-law about his intention of going to Lake Winnipeg with the brigade in spring and proceeding thence to Canada in a bark canoe.

"Of course," said he, "I will take Marie with me, and if you'll take my advice, father, you'll come too."

"No, my son, not yet a while," said old Laroche, shaking his head; "I have a year yet to serve the Company before my engagement is out. After that I may come, if I'm spared; but you know that the Indians are not safe just now, and some of them, I fear, bear me a grudge, for they're a revengeful set."

"That's true, father, but supposin' that all goes well with you, will ye come an' live with Marie and me?"

"We shall see, lad; we shall see," replied Laroche, with a pleased smile; for the old guide evidently enjoyed the prospect of spending the evening of life in the land of his fathers, and under the roof-tree of his son and daughter.

At that moment the report of a gun was heard outside the house. One of the window-panes was smashed and at the same instant Laroche fell heavily forward on the floor.

Jasper sprang up and endeavoured to raise him, but found that he was insensible. He laid him carefully on his back, and hastily opened the breast of his coat. A few drops of blood showed where he had been wounded. Meanwhile several of the men who had been attracted by the gunshot so close to the house burst into the room.

"Stand back, stand back, give him air," cried Jasper; "stay, O God help us! the old man is shot clean through the heart!"

For one moment Jasper looked up with a bewildered glance in the faces of the men, then, uttering a wild cry of mingled rage and agony, he sprang up, dashed them aside, and catching up his gun and snow-shoes rushed out of the house.

He soon found a fresh track in the snow, and the length of the stride, coupled with the manner in which the snow was cast aside, and the smaller bushes were broken and trodden down, told him that the fugitive had made it. In a moment he was following the track with the utmost speed of which he was capable. He never once halted, or faltered, or turned aside, all that day. His iron frame seemed to be incapable of fatigue. He went with his body bent forward, his brows lowering, and his lips firmly compressed; but he was not successful. The murderer had got a sufficiently long start of him to render what sailors call a stern chase a long one. Still Jasper never thought of giving up the pursuit, until he came suddenly on an open space, where the snow had been recently trodden down by a herd of buffaloes, and by a band of Indians who were in chase of them.

Here he lost the track, and although he searched long and carefully he could not find it. Late that night the baffled hunter returned to the fort.

"You have failed — I see by your look," said Mr. Pemberton, as Jasper entered.

"Ay, I have failed," returned the other gloomily. "He must have gone with the band of Indians among whose tracks I lost his footsteps."

"Have you any idea who can have done this horrible deed?" said Pemberton.

"It was Darkeye," said Jasper in a stern voice.

Some of the Indians who chanced to be in the hall were startled, and rose on hearing this.

"Be not alarmed, friends," said the fur-trader. "You are the guests of Christian men. We will not punish you for the deeds of another man of your tribe."

"How does the white man know that this was done by Darkeye?" asked a chief haughtily.

"I *know it*," said Jasper angrily; "I feel sure of it; but I cannot prove it — of course. Does Arrowhead agree with me?"

"He does!" replied the Indian, "and there may be proof. Does Jasper remember the trading store and the *bitten bullet?*"

A gleam of intelligence shot across the countenance of the white hunter as his comrade said this. "True, Arrowhead, true."

He turned, as he spoke, to the body of his late father-in-law, and examined the wound. The ball, after passing through the heart, had lodged in the back, just under the skin.

"See," said he to the Indians, "I will cut out this ball, but before doing so I will tell how I think it is marked."

He then related the incident in the trading store, with which the reader is already acquainted, and afterwards extracted the ball, which, although much flattened and knocked out of shape, showed clearly the deep marks made by the Indian's teeth. Thus, the act which had been done slyly but boastfully before the eyes of a comrade, probably as wicked as himself, became the means whereby Darkeye's guilt was clearly proved.

At once a party of his own tribe were directed by their chief to go out in pursuit of the murderer.

It were vain for me to endeavour to describe the anguish of poor Marie on being deprived of a kind and loving father in so awful and sudden a manner. I will drop a veil over her grief, which was too deep and sacred to be intermeddled with.

On the day following the murder, a band of Indians arrived at Fort Erie with buffalo skins for sale. To the amazement of every one Darkeye himself was among them. The wily savage — knowing that his attempting to quit that part of the country as a fugitive would be certain to fix suspicion on him as the murderer — resolved to face the fur-traders as if he were ignorant of the deed which had been done. By the very boldness of this step he hoped to disarm suspicion; but he forgot the *bitten ball*.

It was therefore a look of genuine surprise that rose to Darkeye's visage, when, the moment he entered the fort, Mr. Pemberton seized him by the right arm, and led him into the hall.

At first he attempted to seize the handle of his knife, but a glance at the numbers of the white men, and the indifference of his own friends, showed him that his best chance lay in cunning.

The Indians who had arrived with him were soon informed by the others of the cause of this, and all of them crowded into the hall to watch the proceedings. The body of poor Laroche was laid on a table, and Darkeye was led up to it. The cunning Indian put on a pretended look of surprise on beholding it, and then the usual expression of stolid gravity settled on his face as he turned to Mr. Pemberton for information.

"*Your* hand did this," said the fur-trader.

"Is Darkeye a dog that he should slay an old man?" said the savage.

"No, you're not a dog," cried Jasper fiercely; "you are worse — a cowardly murderer?"

"Stand back, Jasper," said Mr. Pemberton, laying his hand on the shoulder of the excited hunter, and thrusting him firmly away. "This is a serious charge. The Indian shall not be hastily condemned. He shall have fair play, and *justice*."

"Good!" cried several of the Indians on hearing this. Meanwhile the principal chief of the tribe took up his stand close beside the prisoner.

"Darkeye," said Mr. Pemberton, while he looked stead-fastly into the eyes of the Indian, who returned the look as steadily — "Darkeye, do you remember a conversation you had many weeks ago in the trading store at Jasper's House?"

The countenance of the Indian was instantly troubled, and he said with some hesitation, "Darkeye has had many conversations in that store; is he a medicine-man [a conjurer] that he should know what you mean?"

"I will only put one other question," said the fur-trader. "Do you know this bullet *with the marks of teeth* in it?"

Darkeye's visage fell at once. He became deadly pale, and his limbs trembled. He was about to speak when the chief, who had hitherto stood in silence at his side, suddenly whirled his tomahawk in the air, and, bringing it down on the murderer's skull, cleft him to the chin!

A fierce yell followed this act, and several scalping knives reached the dead man's heart before his body fell to the ground. The scene that followed was terrible. The savages were roused to a state of frenzy, and for a moment the white men feared an attack, but the anger of the Indians was altogether directed against their dead comrade, who had been disliked by his people, while his poor victim Laroche had been a universal favourite. Seizing the body of Darkeye, they carried it down to the banks of the river, hooting and yelling as they went; hacked and cut it nearly to pieces, and then, kindling a large fire, they threw the mangled corpse into it, and burned it to ashes.

It was long before the shadow of this dark cloud passed away from Fort Erie; and it was longer still before poor Marie recovered her wonted cheerfulness. But the presence of Mr. Wilson did much to comfort her. Gradually time softened the pang and healed the wound.

And now, little remains to be told. Winter passed away and spring came, and when the rivers and lakes were sufficiently free from ice, the brigade of boats left Fort Erie, laden with furs, for the sea-coast.

On arriving at Lake Winnipeg, Jasper obtained a small canoe, and, placing his wife and Heywood in the middle of it, he and Arrowhead took the paddles, seated themselves in the bow and stern, and guided their frail bark through many hundreds of miles of wilderness — over many a rough portage, across many a beautiful lake, and up many a roaring torrent, until, finally, they arrived in Canada.

Here Jasper settled. His farm prospered — his family increased. Sturdy boys, in course of time, ploughed the land and blooming daughters tended the dairy. Yet Jasper Derry did not cease to toil. He was one of those men who *feel* that they were made to work, and that much happiness flows from working. He often used to say that if it was God's will, he would "like to die in harness."

Jasper's only weakness was the pipe. It stuck to him and he

stuck to it to the last. Marie, in course of time, came to tolerate it, and regularly filled it for him every night.

Evening was the time when the inmates of Erie Cottage (as their residence was named) enjoyed themselves most; for it was then that the stalwart sons and the blooming daughters circled round the great fire of wood that roared, on winter nights, up the chimney; and it was then that Jasper received his pipe from his still good-looking, though rather stout, Marie, and began to spin yarns about his young days. At this time, too, it was, that the door would frequently open, and a rugged old Indian would stalk in like a mahogany ghost, and squat down in front of the fire. He was often followed by a tall thin old gentleman, who was extremely excitable, but good-humoured. Jasper greeted these two remarkable looking men by the names of Arrowhead and Heywood.

And glad were the young people when they saw their wrinkled faces, for then, they knew from experience, their old father would become more lively than usual, and would go on for hours talking of all the wonders and dangers that he had seen and encountered long, long ago, when he and his two friends were away in the wilderness.

THE END.